Karl, Jean E.

But we are not of
earth

DATE			

But We Are Not of Earth

But We Are
Not of Earth

★─────────────────────★

by JEAN E. KARL

E. P. Dutton   New York

Library of Congress Cataloging in Publication Data

Karl, Jean.   But we are not of earth.

Summary: Four students from Meniscus F delight in the habitable but uninhabited planet they discover until they realize all is not as it seems.
[1. Science fiction]   I. Title.
PZ7.K139Bu   1981   [Fic]   80-21849   ISBN 0-525-27342-5

Published in the United States by Elsevier-Dutton Publishing Co., Inc., 2 Park Avenue, New York, N.Y. 10016

Published simultaneously in Canada by Clarke, Irwin & Company Limited, Toronto and Vancouver

Editor: Ann Durell   Designer: Claire Counihan

Printed in the U.S.A.   First Edition
10 9 8 7 6 5 4 3 2 1

────────────────────────────────────

for all the cousins
with whom I share childhood memories

────────────────────────────────────

1

If your name is Romula Linders, you have to grow up different. Not just because of the Romula—after some antique Earthsider who was reared by an animal! But mostly because of the Linders. And because of what a lot of people know about you.

The Romula, of course, is part of it. I was found by a secondary research team on a scheduled visit to a habitable, but uninhabited, planet; three months old; perfectly content; and with no one else around. My parents, Galsum and Reeabe Linders, were supposed to be there—they were scheduled to meet the research team—but they weren't. Their small ship was there, with me in it, but they were gone. I couldn't have been alone for long, not at three months. Yet no one has seen my parents or heard from them since.

Everything was done to find them. They were too valuable to lose. But no one could discover what had happened. Were they taken away? Or had they taken themselves away somewhere by self-space-placement? It was possible, because in that far part of the galaxy, there were and still are few screens to keep people in or out. But if they did that, why did they go, and where? That was what everyone asked. I certainly didn't know. Not even the mind probers who tested me later were able to take my memory back to three months. Where my parents went or may be is still a mystery.

Which is why I have grown up as an object of curiosity, as well as, if I do say so myself, a valued student, at the Inter-Earth System School and Home for Discoverers' Children. There are other orphans, or presumed orphans, at the school, of course. After all, the Discovery program is dangerous, and people do get lost or killed. But no one with so bizarre a background as mine. The others were left at the school as babies, and their parents disappeared or died later. Some of these disappearances have been odd and unexplained. But only my parents left me elsewhere and vanished.

Did I ever wonder about it? Of course I did! Did I ever get upset? Of course I did! Why would parents leave a three-month-old child to the complete mercy of a secondary research team and the School/Home if they cared anything at all about her? There was no evidence that they had met with abductors or even an accident. So what could I think but that they didn't want me, didn't care enough to take me along wherever they went? It's a depressing thought, the idea that your own parents did not want you. But I'd lived with it a long time, and I'd learned to accept it, though not to like it.

So where does that leave me? It means that the

2

School/Home is responsible for me until I'm twenty-one—or until I find gainful employment—just as it is for all the others, whether their parents are alive or dead. But for me, for years, it also meant that endless quantities of people came to try to find something in me that would tell where my parents had gone. None of which was designed to find my parents alone. As I said, other Discoverers have disappeared under odd circumstances, and I am, or was, the only clue to any of them.

But enough of that, enough of my parents. I was once sure that I would never do what they had done. Now I am no longer so certain. I am my parents' daughter. I have proved that to myself and to others in an adventure I am still trying to sort out in my mind. In fact, that's what this book is about—that adventure and what it has come to mean to me and to my friends.

At the School/Home, we live in pods, four or five of us to a group. The pods for children up to eleven are all in one area, and there's an adult in each pod. When you are eleven, you are transferred to another section where there's an adult for two or three pods, living nearby. And finally, when you're in your late teens, you live in a section where there's only one adult for the whole area.

For almost my entire life, I have shared a pod with the same three friends, the ones who also shared my great adventure. We have always been known as The Terrible Four, a fact of which we are rather proud. It gives us a certain distinction. Though we are also distinguished by the fact that we are the only pod in which

3

the parents of every member are either missing or dead.

At the time of our adventure, we were in the middle group. Caper Jenicks had been the adult with our pod ever since we moved into that section. He had two other pods, and sometimes he said he was glad the other two weren't like us. But we knew he liked us just the same. Most of the time he could even manage to laugh about us.

We are definitely a mixed pod: two boys and two girls. The other girl is Bisty Halab. Her parents were lost in Sector 21, exploring the ruins of a vanished civilization. The two boys are Waver Wistrow and Gloust Torgund. Waver's parents are thought to have been killed when their ship got too near a nova they had been sent out to check. Gloust has been told that his folks disappeared on a secret mission near the galactic center. So that's the four of us.

We are really quite different from each other, which may be why we have always gotten along so well and have been able to think up so many marvelous things to do. The School/Home is essentially boring. It is totally Discovery-oriented, and no one thinks of anything else. Which is why it sometimes needs the sort of stirring up we like to give it.

The problem is that there is no place for any of us here to go except into Discovery. Earth likes to keep to itself. Many years ago—thousands of years ago—there was what the Earth people call The Clordian Sweep. Most people on Earth were killed in that attack by another planet. Those who lived were changed, and the new civilization that grew up kept a low profile; even when other planets were friendly, the Earth did not welcome newcomers.

4

When it became evident that Earth people had a special ability to move themselves from one place to another, and to control ships by a special mind-power, Earth began to help other planets explore the galaxy. But the people who left Earth to do this were not allowed to return. Everyone at our base had either left Earth themselves, or their parents or grandparents had left; and none of us were allowed to go to Earth. Minded inhabitants of other planets could go to the Earth for meetings, and some Earth people could leave on government business and go back. But we would never be allowed to set foot on the place. Our lives would have to be lived on Discovery bases, all of which were set up on basically uninhabitable planets. Earth does not colonize either.

But that's all history. The important thing is that we four, and every other child at the School/Home, were destined for Discovery. There was no other place for us in Earth's plans. And there was no other inhabited planet where we would feel at home, for other minded species seemed, always, very different from us when it came to living with them. And even if you think Discovery itself may be exciting, learning about it can be dull and routine.

Because of the way we felt, because we sometimes thought we couldn't endure another stodgy School/Home day without exploding, we four were more than excited, we were ecstatic when the School/Home announced a new program. It was supposed to provide more challenge, more growing and learning experiences, for middle-group students. Obviously it was made for us. The only problem was that we weren't at all sure we would be included.

5

The truth is that we were in more disgrace than usual. We had— But I guess I can't tell you about that until you know a little more about us and the School/Home. The source of most of our difficulties—The Terrible Four—was that we liked to try new ideas, and sometimes they didn't quite work the way we'd planned. We never really meant to get into trouble. It was just that our ideas didn't always fit into the regular Discovery patterns.

Education patterns in the school are quite rigid. We all learn communication in mixed societies, galactic geography, space math, and all that sort of thing. And of course we learn to fly ships, mostly in stationary trainers. The only really useless classes are those in Earth history, geography and culture. But since we are of Earth descent, the School/Home thinks we ought to know what Earth is like.

Beyond the things that everyone takes, there are the specialties. By the time we have moved into the middle section, most of us have been fitted into one of the four Discovery paths: ship development, manufacture and maintenance; ship navigation and planet identification; life-support systems—human maintenance in space; and planetary research—classification and exploration of other bodies. Sometimes you can work at more than one. I was taking courses in both the first and second. Bisty was, and still is, an absolute genius at life-support systems. Gloust was mostly involved in planet exploration techniques. Waver, who may be the brightest of us all, was bored by everything. Officially he was learning navigation—and he was good at it. But what he really liked was just learning. Somehow he had managed to find some book cards that had been sent to the base by accident, and he spent half his time with them—reading pre–Clordian Sweep poets and philosophers. Talk about useless knowledge! If he hadn't always known all the answers in all the classes he went to, he might have been the despair of the entire School/Home. As it was, the teachers just hoped he'd grow out of it and settle down to a distinguished Discovery career.

So there we were, all settled into our Discovery paths and hating the awful predictability of them, when this great new opportunity struck. The challenge had to do with the small, medium-range ships that we had been learning to fly. Those selected for the new program would be sent on special missions. We had only recently gotten to the point at which we were allowed to take short trips away from the base in training ships, and the thought of a longer trip was positively explosive. Yet, ironically, it was because of one of our short training trips that we were in trouble.

We liked flying, maybe because controlling a ship is not easy. Anyone can make one go. But making it arrive where you want it to arrive is something else. Computers don't do it all. It takes careful planning and determined concentration under the thought-drive helmet to get where you're going.

The first four or five times we four directed a ship, the main navithought teacher took us out. That's Frecka Umberst. She's a riser. We never had any trouble with her. But then when we were ready for our next try, we learned that our passenger-teacher would be Keery Soter. She sometimes came to be our pod mentor when Caper Jenicks had to be away, and as such, she was something less than a favorite. As a teacher, we thought she was even worse. Keery Soter's problem, we had decided, was that she thought she knew everything. And through the years we four had taken great pains to teach her that this was not true. Unfortunately, she had proved to be a slow learner. Our little efforts to help her had never succeeded. It was too bad! She would be so much nicer, we felt, if she would only realize that she had a few flaws in her information system.

The teacher on a navithought training trip is not supposed to do anything. Just watch. And, of course, break in if there is real trouble. A destination is set, and the training crew is supposed to clamp into the helmets and take the ship there and back in a specific amount of time. You can't make a lot of mistakes going or coming and get back in the time limit.

On this sixth trip we were going to Claudius C, in the 10th Sector. Claudius C is an Earth Discovery base, but unlike ours, it is not a School/Home and Discoverers' base; instead it is a shipbuilding base. The planet is, of course, not a habitable one. The base is underground, like ours; and the people there mine the elements they need for the ships, as well as build them. The only thing they have to import is food, and they probably grow some of that, too, in specially lighted sections.

At any rate, the trip there certainly did not promise any excitement—no new vistas. What it did involve were two stop breaks, our first. We had been taught to do breaks, and we'd been through them as passengers. Nothing about the process was a surprise. But it was the new thing for us to do on the trip. We thought it was hardly worth the trouble.

At least we did until we discovered something very interesting when we were checking the navicharts. The usual flight pattern from our planet to Claudius C makes a short jump at a field focus of 80 degrees, then a straight burst for a clear field spot at 20 degrees, and finally a coast at 15 degrees for the planet itself. This is a clear route. No strong gravitational fields that might mean black holes without the usual accretion disks; no gamma sources that might mean antimatter. Very safe. Very sure. Very well traveled. Very stodgy. Which is why it's the route usually used for this level trip.

But we had noticed that there was a field curve focus at about 40 degrees that would eliminate the need for one stop. We could take the curve; then at a given point, we could break and jump right to Claudius C. It seemed safe. None of the charts showed anything in the way. No one seemed to have taken the route or checked it out specifically, but the general area had been well authenticated. So that was the course we decided to use.

Needless to say, we did not discuss our plans with Keery Soter. This was to be another of her little lessons in learning.

Well, not to keep you wondering if we killed ourselves and her, too, may I say that we did not. On the day of the trip, we got ourselves under the helmet, synched our minds, and were off. Keery Soter was busy being prim and distant in the background. Passengers can't talk to people under the helmet, and although navithought drive isn't as instantaneous as self-space-placement, it is quick. So a teacher doesn't have much chance to change things.

When the time that would normally bring the first stop break arrived, of course we weren't ready for one. Our single break would come a few minutes later. We knew just where we were. But Keery Soter went crazy. She kept making all sorts of wild motions, which we ignored. We knew what we were doing, even if she didn't. She tried to make one of us give up a helmet, but of course not one of us did. We pushed on, came to our breakpoint, made it, changed course, and arrived at Claudius C at least ten minutes early.

As we took off our helmets, we met the storm. Who did we think we were? What had we done? We showed her, but that didn't help. She obviously did not approve of new and faster routes.

The workers at the base on Claudius C were surprised to see us so soon, but they only laughed when we told them what we'd done. Keery Soter, though, wouldn't go back with us. She said she was sure we were going to run that ship into oblivion. The people at the base didn't know what to do. They couldn't spare anyone to go back with us. So they gave us the paper we had to have, to show we'd been there, and then turned their backs while we took off alone. We got back fifteen minutes ahead of the fastest schedule, and without Keery Soter.

It was awkward all around: first, because no one else had ever discovered that more direct route; second, because we hadn't done what we were really supposed to do; and third, because now someone had to go for Keery Soter. Who would never forgive us, we realized all too late. Which didn't seem quite fair. After all, we had been in charge of getting us there and back, and we had. We'd done it in great style.

Somehow it had never occurred to us that such a simple thing would get us into trouble. But it did! Outrage everywhere! And that very same day the announcement was made of the new program.

Unfortunately, our pod mentor, Caper Jenicks, was away. He usually taught space health and nutrition at the School/Home. But really he was a plant and plant-equivalent specialist. He and his wife had been Discoverers, but he had received a leg injury that still bothered him, and she had been killed when they landed on a planet where the plant life grew at incredible speeds. Since then, he had gone on missions only occasionally. We longed to talk with him and hoped he would be back that night, as planned.

But when he came in, he was no help. Like most of the other teachers, he seemed to think we had committed the one unpardonable crime, though no one would tell us just what it was that we had done wrong. So we could only hope that Caper would see it in another light when he had had a chance to rest, and would come to our defense. He always came home from Discovery trips in a grouchy, distant sort of mood, so there was reason for optimism. In the meantime, we listened to his lecture and had to admit, even to ourselves, that we were in deep trouble. Everyone at the School/Home seemed to be convinced that we couldn't be trusted.

It was very discouraging. The first new thing that had ever happened at the dreary old School/Home, and we might not be allowed to go. Worried? We were frantic! We couldn't remember anything in all our lives that we had ever wanted so much. The more we thought about it, the more the new program seemed the only way out of the daily dullness in which we were immersed. The program could have blasted us out of the galaxy forever and we wouldn't have cared. We wanted it, whatever it turned out to be.

2

Each pod at the School/Home has two bedrooms and a pod-center room. Our pod-center room was always full of kids from other middle-section pods. The day after our disaster, when our classes were out, we had more visitors than usual. Some of them wanted to find out just what we had done on the way to Claudius C. The rest had just heard that we had some kind of problem and wanted to gloat. Of course, the conversation eventually turned to the new program, but no one knew any more about it than we did. Some wanted to go, and some didn't. Not all potential Discoverers are big on Discovery. Some would prefer a more settled future.

The talk dwindled finally because we four didn't want to talk about Claudius C, and about the other we all had too little knowledge. You can't say the same thing very many times before it gets boring.

So finally Gloust got up and said, as only he can, "Why don't you all go now? If you stay too long, there might be guilt by association. You're safer out of here."

Everyone laughed, but they knew Gloust meant it about leaving. So they went. And we four were left to lay some plans.

"I'm not as desperate as the rest of you for diversion," Bisty began. "But a trip to anywhere would certainly give me a chance to test some of the things Foker Wand and I have been working on. We have a new locking mechanism for thought-drive helmets that we think could save a life in an emergency, and a new kind of oxygen equipment."

Gloust grunted. "Forget your stupid inventions for a minute, Bisty, if you can. The important thing is to find a way to move out of here."

Sometimes Gloust can be too blunt, but right then I was glad to have him keep us on course. Bisty may be the bright hope of life-support systems, and we all know that space survival is one of the most difficult disciplines taught at the School, but frankly, testing out new devices was not my idea, either, of why we needed the trip.

"Don't get so excited," Waver said. "You're all too worried. Of course we'll go."

"You weren't so sure last night," I muttered. "In my opinion, it would be just like them not to let us go, if for no other reason than to 'protect us.' "

"Look, Rom," Waver said patiently, "think about it another way. Remember they don't really know what to do with us. They're not against us, not most of them. Just perplexed by us. They may have invented this whole thing just to get us, and maybe a few of the others, out of here for a while."

Gloust nodded. Then changed his mind and shook his head. "Don't count on it."

"I wish I really knew what they were thinking," Bisty said. "There are some things I'd like to get ready if we are going somewhere."

"Listen," Waver said, "don't be so dense. They have to let us go. If for no other reason than to convince us that we have limitations."

We were all quiet a moment. Caper had said something the night before in his lecture about realizing our limitations, but I had thought our limitations were all imposed by the School/Home. Obviously Waver thought otherwise. Or did he?

"You mean they might want us to go and fail?" I asked. "I don't see how we could fail at any reasonable thing they asked us to do. And if we did, wouldn't they look bad, too?"

"Maybe. And maybe not," Waver said. "It makes sense. Think about it."

"Like we were doing with Keery Soter," Bisty murmured.

"Of course, and for almost the same reason," Waver said. "The only trouble is that the basic setup is different. We could lose by going. Keery Soter never had anything to lose but her stupidity."

"You may be right," Gloust admitted. "I never thought of it that way. But I want to go anyway. I don't care what happens. I just want to go."

I nodded, though I did care what happened. I didn't want to get lost in space or find myself studying something I hated because we had been tricked into something too hard for us.

"Can we just think it's going to happen then?" Bisty asked, still dubious.

"Well, no," said Waver. "I thought we might talk to Caper. He's generally on the committees that plan this sort of thing. And he might put in a good word for us if he's cooled down since yesterday."

That was the first suggestion we had had for action, and we fell on it. Caper was always in a better mood the day after he came back from a trip than he was on the day he arrived, so it was worth a try at least. It only took us two minutes to decide to look for him.

He had hidden himself in one of the farthest reaches of our underground base, and he didn't seem altogether delighted to see us. He still had some of that abstracted, gloomy look. But still, we took a chance

"What about the new program?" Gloust asked, hardly waiting to say hello. "We want to be sure we're chosen for it."

"Naturally you want to go," Caper said, and added with, I thought, unnecessary irony, "Navithought propulsion is such a strong skill with you four—not to mention advanced charting—that of course the entire universe needs the benefits of your exploring abilities immediately."

That wasn't like Caper. He didn't generally keep coming back to things. But at the same time a grin flashed over his face, and it gave me hope.

"Caper, we have to go," I said. "We need the experience. And besides there's nothing to do here."

"Nonsense. Your problem is that at fourteen you've

16

had too many experiences, all of you. You need peace and reevaluation."

"Oh, Caper!" Bisty sounded as irritated as I felt. "Don't talk like Keery Soter. We counted on you."

Caper was almost smiling now—or maybe laughing at us. But no matter, he seemed to be coming around to our point of view, and that was what counted. "What do you want me to do?"

"Speak for us at the committee," Waver said quickly.

"What shall I tell them?"

"Oh, you know," Waver said. "All about our needing to learn our limitations and that sort of thing. How the trip will give us a new perspective on our inadequacies: make us feel small in the universe."

Caper laughed outright then. "You may be right," he said. And we knew then that he would do his best for us. In fact, I had a feeling he had always intended to see that we went, sooner or later. He had just been teasing us.

"Then you will help us," Gloust concluded.

"If I possibly can," he said, very firmly. And he looked as if he wanted us to go as much as we did.

We had thought that doing something to achieve our goal would relieve our minds. Make us more confident. But it didn't. If anything, it made us more anxious, now that there was reason to hope.

At the School/Home, the pattern for classes is eight days of work and then a three-day pause. Our planet, Meniscus F, is one that has long, long days and long, long nights. But since we live and work underground, days and nights have simply been set on an Earthlike

17

pattern that bears no relationship to those of the planet itself. Most Earth bases are set up that way; it helps people adjust when they move from base to base.

The day after we saw Caper was the last day of the work octave. We almost didn't go to classes, we were so anxious. But then we decided that that was not a good idea. Instead we needed to become model students. Show that we could be trusted. So that's what we set out to do.

We played it like a game. Each of us became, in one way or another, a model of what the perfect School/ Home student ought to be. In fact, we went far beyond the limits of our tolerance for that kind of nonsense.

In spite of the fact that Bisty was already busy working with Foker Wand, the head of Life Support at the base, on all kinds of new inventions, the curriculum for Life Support called for her to be in a basic elementary space equipment class. So there she was, busy learning what she seemed to have been born knowing. And generally she resented it and was not very kind to anyone in the class. But that day she actually let the teacher help her make one of those simple, all-purpose space garments for planets of unknown atmosphere. Bisty hates making that sort of thing. It's elementary and stupid as far as she's concerned. But she knows that teachers like to feel helpful now and then, and like to be able to do things for you—show you what they know. So she played helpless, and the teacher glowed with delight.

Gloust spent the day talking, instead of responding in grunts and diagrams. And when someone in his planet-survey planning class said he would set up a tent on a planet that Gloust knew had to be mostly gas, he didn't laugh out loud, just grinned quietly and suggested that

18

the tent be moved to the inside of one of those little survey modules.

Waver did not mention abstract mathematical theory, T. S. Eliot, John Locke, or even his favorite, Shakespeare, all day. In his three-dimensional charting class, he actually let someone else answer a question about a theory involving four-dimensional aspects of intergalactic charting. All of which must have overwhelmed Reesta Greet, the teacher, although she likes theory almost as much as Waver.

As for me, I was sweet and charming to everyone, or at least I tried to be. I even helped some dolt repair a small telescope he had taken apart, sweetly explaining why the pieces had to fit together as they did.

It was difficult beyond belief for all of us. We wondered that we survived the day.

We were all stretched out on the floor of our pod-center room, staring at the ceiling, when Caper came in, then just stood there and laughed.

"I don't know which is harder to deal with, the old Terrible Four or the new paragons of virtue. I don't really think any of you is going to die if you don't get sent on one of those missions. But I think the whole school may die of overkindness and reasonableness if you stay around."

"What does that mean?" Gloust muttered.

"It means that the faculty committee is afraid not to send you. They don't want to be responsible for the consequences to the rest of us if you have to stay here."

We all sat up.

"That's not very polite," I said. "We were just trying to be what everyone thinks we ought to be."

"It will never work," Caper said. "You don't have the

minds for it. But don't worry. You won't have to go through a day like this again. At least not soon."

At that point we really began to listen. It sounded as if we might actually be going.

"Are the lists out?" Bisty asked cautiously.

"They are. And here's one—with your names prominently featured. As a matter of fact, you are to be the first. The test cases. The school can't get you out of here fast enough."

"Do you really mean it?" Waver demanded, snatching the list from Caper.

"Where's all that sweet agreeableness?" Caper asked. "I knew it would disappear, but I did think you might at least hold out through the day. So it wouldn't look quite so put-on."

"Oh, Caper, don't be such a wall," I said. "You know we were trying to prove we could do things right. And I think we did pretty well. Now quit railing at us and tell us about the trip. When are we going? And what's it supposed to be?"

"I just had to prove to myself that you were the same old brutal beasts inside. Now that I have, let me sit down and give you the worst."

"Brutal beasts!" exclaimed Bisty. "If I weren't so grateful to you, I'd throw you out."

"We're the best this School/Home has to offer," Waver told him solemnly.

"A modest group," said Caper. "But look here, you four, you'd better let me explain."

"By all means do so," said Waver. "We're waiting. Just don't think we cannot be hurt by insult. We have tender sensibilities, and if you continue to tread on

20

them, how can you expect us not to respond in kind?"

Caper laughed again. "It's the School that's responding in kind. You like to explore. So you're going to."

"Just the four of us?" I said, excited.

"The four of you, and, may the stars protect me, your old pod mentor, Caper," he announced.

We all looked at each other in surprise.

"Oh, Caper," Bisty said. "Really?"

"That's sensational," I said. "I was sure if we got to go and there had to be an adult, we would get Keery Soter. Though I don't suppose she'd want it any more than we would," I added.

"But why do we have to have an adult at all?" asked Waver. "I thought this was something new—a challenge."

"Don't you want me?" Caper asked.

"Aren't you afraid?" Waver said.

"Terrified," Caper said. "But then Discoverers learn to live with fear."

We all laughed. It was a phrase we had heard endlessly.

"Where are we going, and when?" Gloust asked.

"You are going after the next two octaves and two pauses. And where you go depends on you. The faculty has decided to make each of these missions different. Some will be harder than others. But yours is a sort of mystery jaunt. You, my friends, and I, too, of course, are going on a survival mission."

"A survival mission!" We looked at each other. What did that mean?

"Just retribution, my friends. As I said before. You sometimes make the faculty members here wonder if they will survive. And now you will work to survive yourselves. Oh, don't look so doubtful. I'm sure you will."

But it wasn't doubtful that I was feeling. Only surprised.

"Just what is it, Caper?" I asked.

"I'm trying to explain. Your project is based on a kind of testing or toughening process they used on Earth long ago. One or two young people were left in a wild area to survive on their own for a couple of days or even a couple of weeks sometimes."

"You mean we'll be taken out and left someplace?" Gloust asked. "I thought we were going to fly a ship."

"Oh, you'll fly a ship all right," Caper said. "A pretty one, too. One of those fancy new jobs, a Q101."

"A Q101!" I gasped. The base had only one Q101, and I had never even seen the outside of it. It had been designed for moderate-length research trips and took four under the helmet like our usual trainer. But it was far more modern than anything we had ever used. I had heard that there might be one coming that would be used as a trainer, but I could hardly believe that they would give it to us for our trip. "Why would they do something as marvelous as that—giving us a Q101?"

"Wait until you hear the rest," Caper said.

"What else could matter?" I asked.

"A lot," Caper answered. And I thought he looked pleased. "We'll take the ship, a limited amount of supplies, a certain amount of gear, and we'll be gone for at least three octaves and the pauses between. During that time you will have to visit at least three planets and find at least one habitable planet where we can get

22

food, water and oxygen. It will be your job to survive on your own."

"What kinds of planets?" Gloust asked.

"They must be uninhabited," Caper explained. "And, of course, planets you can land the ship on."

"Uninhabited!" Gloust couldn't believe it. "There aren't any we can land on in moderate range, let alone any that would supply us with food, water and oxygen."

"Are you sure?" Caper asked with a grin.

"I'll have to check. But I don't remember any."

"There are none known in any of the nearby sectors," Waver said, out of his infinite memory.

"Does that mean we can go beyond moderate range?" Gloust asked. "Will the ship take us far enough?"

"All the way to Sector 22, if you want," Caper said. "You'll be getting more complete instructions as soon as they can be prepared."

"Do they really want us to go so far away?" I asked. Maybe the School/Home was just testing our common sense, I thought.

"Not if you can find what you need nearby," Caper said.

But the implication was that we wouldn't. It all sounded a little odd, and even dangerous. Yet surely the School/Home wouldn't deliberately endanger us or Caper, or the Q101. And it would be glorious to be exploring on our own. Especially in a ship like that!

"Tell us once more," Waver said. "What kinds of planets are we supposed to find?"

"Uninhabited. Wild. Yet supportive of life. And we have to bring back location charts."

"The faculty committee decided this?" Bisty asked.

She was clearly bothered. This was going to give her more of a chance to test her latest inventions than she had wanted, I thought. Bisty had never been big on travel.

Caper nodded again.

"With such faith and trust behind us, how can we fail," Waver announced. "And Caper knows all about edibles."

"Which is why I insisted on going," Caper said. "To save you if you get into too much trouble." He gave us a sly grin.

Hadn't they planned to send an adult along then? Was the trip originally planned just for the training crew? But that didn't make sense. This trip was beginning to sound like the Discovery trips our parents had made, not a school jaunt. And even if we had overstepped ourselves a bit on that trip to Claudius C, the staff surely knew that we hadn't been on any really long-distance trips, not even as passengers. Maybe it wasn't as difficult a trip as Caper had described. And surely, I thought, an adult had been planned. Caper had just volunteered to be that adult.

"We'll get you back safe, Caper," I said protectively.

"We'll even let you help," Waver assured him.

Caper grinned again. "I'm always willing to be consulted. And don't think you can fool me as easily as you did Keery Soter when you do your planning. But if I were you, I wouldn't start deciding just what you're going to do until you see the whole thing written out for you. That'll be sometime early in the next octave. And it would probably be best if you didn't talk too much about the trip until you do know exactly what you'll have to do."

24

When Caper left, we looked at each other in awe. We were going, and it would be far more of a trip than we had dreamed possible.

"I'm glad we're going," I said. "But it's not going to be a vacation."

"It's getting away," Gloust said. "We'll be out of this black hole for a while. That's what's important."

"And when haven't we been able to take care of ourselves?" Bisty said. "Though I really don't need that much of a trip to test my new oxygen equipment and helmet locks. Still, it may be interesting."

"So it's off from the wasteland into wonderland," Waver shouted.

And we all laughed. If any of us harbored a corner of fear, we ignored it. There had always been a successful way out of everything. And besides, we had two whole octaves to get ready. In that time we could do a lot of preparing for whatever might happen.

3

The whole school was talking about our trip by the next morning. Our names had been posted as the first group to go, and everyone came by, wanting to know all about it. But we didn't have much to tell. In the first place, we didn't know very much ourselves; and then, Caper had said not to mention what we did know. So we just said vague things about being gone for three octaves and the pauses between. And we explained that we were to get detailed information later. That seemed to satisfy most people, and those it didn't were only jealous. So we rubbed it in a little. What would the School/Home do without us for three whole octaves! And there we would be, lazing around the galaxy. It sounded good. I only hoped it would prove to be that pleasant.

That was the first of the three pause days. By the end of the pause, our very reticence, our casualness—and of course our mild boasting—had made us the envy of the whole School/Home. And with that envy came a greater measure of self-confidence for us. We had convinced ourselves that we could handle whatever the faculty committee threw at us. Wild places anywhere in the galaxy would provide mere holidays for us. No matter what the motives of the faculty might be in sending us off on such a jaunt, we could do what was asked and come home in triumph. After all, how bad could it be? And besides, Caper would be there if some emergency did arise.

When the new octave began, we waited anxiously, but not fearfully, for the detailed instructions from the committee. We assumed they would call us in and talk with us, but no message came from the committee. There was nothing we could do but wait.

It was late afternoon on that first day of the new octave. We four were gathered in our pod-center room, wondering what would happen next, when Caper came in. He carried a few papers and waved them at us.

"The instructions, Caper, old friend?" Waver asked. "Or just the preliminaries?"

"Oh, the whole thing," Caper said.

"Then we don't have to see the committee," I said.

"No," said Caper. "They decided that I could take care of whatever was needed. I'm here to answer your questions, provide solace and comfort, and in general supervise—as well as go along, of course."

"And have you decided that we'll bring you through, or are you still terror stricken?" Waver asked.

"I've never been worried about me," Caper said with a sudden grin. "It's you I've been worried about. What will happen, I keep thinking, to that poor boy when all his theories have been tested and he finds they're all wrong? What will happen when he discovers that pre–Clordian Sweep philosophy has no place on wild planets? But I've decided to let it happen with no gloomy presentiments from me."

"I'm glad you've made such a wise decision," Waver said. "I may not know much about wild planets, but a good philosophy fits anywhere. And there is no such word as *failure* in my philosophy!"

"Not in your philosophy, perhaps. But the faculty may have plans for your actions that will defeat you. They may think you need to discover that you have a few flaws in your information system. It might make you easier to live with."

We all laughed, even Waver.

"What about you?" Bisty asked. "You're a part of this. Do you need to learn about your flaws, too?"

"No, I'll be there to report yours," Caper retorted.

"This is all talk," I said. "Let's see those instructions. How can we tell how ignominious our failures will be if we don't even know what we're expected to do?"

Caper held out the paper, and we all crowded around. The instructions were brief and contained little we did not already know:

The space team will leave with the following:

    One Q101 space navithought ship
    Equipment for all-planet space suit construction
    One basic field guide book on each of the following:
        galactic navigation
        rock and mineral identification
        moderate-range planet identification
        keys to edible materials
        illness and space medicine

space exercise
space health
disaster techniques
The usual basic navigation charts
Standard Q101 disaster and medical supplies
Food for four days
Oxygen for six days
Water for six days

The space team will be gone for three full octaves and the intermediate pauses, returning at any time during the third pause or a day or two thereafter. An earlier return, or a much later return, will be evidence of failure, and the team will be recommended for further study in the necessary areas, based on the ship's log of the time spent away and other evidence. At least three different planets are to be visited, and the team must secure supplies when and where they can. No space credits will be issued, although necessary charges will be honored once accounted for.

If the team is successful, appropriate steps will be taken, after a full report of the journey, to build on the experience with advanced studies.

I think all of us were appalled by the starkness of the instructions. Nothing about the trip would be easy.

"What they want us to do is clear enough," Bisty said. "But what do those last two paragraphs mean?"

"They mean," Caper said, "that if you don't do what they ask, find the proper kinds of uninhabited planets and survive on them, you are doomed to what I am sure the four of you might call dullness. Repetition and re-education, you might say. And if you succeed, you may just get some harder courses. But more likely you will be sent out again on an even more difficult mission. Go until you fail seems to be the message."

"Is this all because of what we did to Keery Soter?" Gloust asked.

"I don't think you ever realized what a dangerous enemy Keery Soter can be," Caper said. "I should have warned you. I thought I had. And I never dreamed you'd make such a fool of her, or do such a crazy thing as taking a new way to Claudius C when she was aboard your ship. However, it may not be as bad as it sounds. Not everyone on the committee agrees that the trip should be this difficult. If you succeed, there may be those who will speak for you."

"How comforting you are, Caper," Waver said. "Shall we give up now while we still have some energy left?"

"You may give up, Waver," I said. "But I won't. If nothing else, we have to go because we're going to get to use a Q101. Don't forget that."

"No, for goodness sakes don't give up before you start," Caper said. "I'll give you all the help and advice I can—all I'm allowed to give. We'll work it out. You'll come through. And you can face what comes next when this trip is over."

We nodded and looked at the instructions again.

"Why doesn't it say here in the basic design that the planets have to be uninhabited?" Bisty asked.

"That's understood," Caper said. "After all, this is called a survival mission."

"And three planets," I said. "They couldn't be content with our finding one?"

"If we find one that supplies the food, water, and oxygen we need, we can always make our base there and simply make quick trips to a couple of other less hospitable planets," Caper said.

"Then all of the planets we go to don't have to be completely habitable planets?" Gloust said.

"No, I never said they did," Caper answered.

"The ship must have oxygen renewing and storing equipment, but not constant supply facilities," I said. "It will carry enough, I suppose, for six days, since that's what we're being given. And water tanks for six days' supply, which can be refilled."

"We might have to get water in one place and oxygen in another," Bisty murmured. "Although any food we can eat would probably require the presence, in some form, of both. Will the equipment do some purification, if necessary?"

"It will," I said. "We went over some of the basic Q101 equipment in repair class. But I never thought I'd see one so soon."

"Then I guess we have nothing to worry about, after all," Waver said. "Six days is a long time. And we've got good equipment. We can get anywhere and back in six days. Why be upset?"

Theoretically, he was right. But practically, I wasn't so sure. Still, I knew we would certainly make the best of it. Whatever happened, we would do our best to succeed.

4

We found we were expected to go to our regular classes for the next two octaves; so we did, at least until the last few days. Our exercise in being friendly and helpful was over, of course. But what took its place must have been almost as agreeable. We were abstracted. Our minds were not where our bodies were, and we created almost no disruptions. At the same time, we did the work we were asked to do because we didn't want any trouble or extra assignments. Most of it was stuff we could toss off pretty easily. And by helping each other and planning well, we managed to create whole chunks of time for getting organized and for practicing. We did not intend to get caught short for lack of effort.

There were five things we had to do: perfect our teamwork under the helmet; decide where we were going first; learn everything the ship and its equipment could do; get ourselves in top physical condition; and get together our supplies.

Through all of our getting ready, Caper was not around. He didn't usually go off on long Discovery trips, and certainly not two so close together, but an emergency mission came up, one that needed his specialty, and he left in a hurry the day after we got our instructions. We were upset, and he seemed even more disturbed than we were. Of course, the inevitable Keery Soter came to take over in his place. We thought the School/Home could have done better, just that once. It wouldn't have hurt them to find someone else. But there she was. We ignored her as much as we could. And she ignored us, which was the one bright spot in the whole big mess. All this meant, however, that there was no one to answer any questions we had about our mission. Caper had been our liaison. We couldn't ask Keery Soter anything. And no one else seemed to have been appointed to take Caper's place.

It made us angry at first, the thought that the School/Home would send us off on such a difficult trip and not give us any help at all in getting ready. But then we decided that no matter what they thought of us, or what they were planning for us on this trip, we were going to succeed, and we would do it on our own, if that's what they wanted. We knew we had to check off certain things with the committee before we went, but until then we would do our planning and our preparation by ourselves.

Part of every day we spent in the small, stationary navithought trainers. One of these had been reserved for our use in the training center—we could have it whenever we wanted it. And Frecka Umberst always seemed to be there when we were. She helped us hone down our group control until we were like one large brain when we got under the helmets together.

The fact that we knew each other so well helped. And of course, four is an advantage. You really have to know what you're doing when you take out one of the two-thought-drive ships that are used by small Discovery teams. We still had a way to go before any of us would be ready for that. But we knew Frecka Umberst was pleased with the amount of control and drive we were able to manage.

The decision on where to go proved to be more of a problem. We were able to secure the charts we would be allowed to take with us, of course. They included most of the sectors of the galaxy, though not the core; we would have no equipment along that would allow us to survive there. We checked first for planets in the sectors around us that might have what we needed. Most of the ones nearby that we could land on, and certainly any known to have food, water or oxygen, had indigenous minded life or had been put to some kind of use by someone else. Any others tended to be totally hostile. Increasingly, finding a destination seemed a puzzle with no solution. We spent hours over the charts and got nowhere. And we were left with no time for learning about the ship or amassing supplies.

"Look," Waver said finally. "This is no good. We're not getting ready fast enough. We have to split up and work on different things, except at the trainer and maybe in fitness training."

None of us could quarrel with that. We had all begun to see that two octaves was very little time in which to organize the knowledge we needed to handle the trip well.

"I'll see if I can get some plans for the ship and study them," I offered. We wouldn't be allowed to get on the ship until a day or two before we were to leave. And the Q101 was a little different from the trainers we were used to. Since ship maintenance was one of my specialties, it made sense for me to study the ship and its equipment, and tell the others what they needed to know. In fact, I could hardly wait to begin.

Gloust, it was decided, would learn how to determine planetary natures from the information provided by scanners, and how to cope physically with the varied sorts of planets we might find ourselves landing on. He was also in charge of our fitness training. It was up to him to find out just how strong we needed to be to survive in the wild. He was the only one of us really looking forward to coping with a totally alien environment.

Waver, who loved to cope with the past, as long as it provided new ideas, was sent off to read old reports of trips to unknown planets. We hoped that research of that sort would turn up some likely landing spots. And we knew that, if nothing else, he would come up with some odd facts about little-known places in the galaxy, information that might prove useful. Fortunately, Waver was as good at math as he was at poetry and philosophy, so he could be trusted to find any possible planets on the galactic chart.

Bisty was to check out all of our life-support systems—the gear and the food we would be allowed to take. And she was also, along with Gloust, supposed to get some information on the basic problems we might face in trying to live on unexplored, untested planets.

This, along with information about the extremes of environment we could endure, both with and without the several kinds of space suits our ship would allow us to produce, would determine how successful our little colony would be—providing, of course, that we actually found planets we could exist on at all.

After we set up this division, we met at specific times each day for helmet training and fitness training, but spent the rest of our free time on our own specialties.

Fitness training was something only Gloust had ever taken seriously before. But now we all realized that we might get into situations that would call for sheer physical endurance. So every day he had us running on treadmills, with pictures of Earth scenery flashing in front of us, and doing exercises on our backs with a simulated sky and cloud movement above our heads. It seemed strange to think that before too long we might be doing some of the same thing with real scenery around us. None of us could quite imagine what this would be like.

We compared notes before we went to bed each night, and our plans seemed to be working. By the fourth day of the second octave, we had amassed a lot of information in every area. But our main problem still had not been solved—where to go first. We still did not know where to find the kind of planet we needed.

We pored over the charts together one night, and went over the information Waver had uncovered. In various reports, he had found an amazing number of planets that had been visited only once and had never been put on the general navigation charts. Some of these planets sounded promising.

"What we really need, though," he said, "is not an

isolated planet, but an area where there might be more than one to explore. It would make things a lot easier for us."

We all agreed with that, but there didn't seem to be any place like that available—at least not near. But then we didn't have to stay near, did we? I began to think back then, and I remembered something Caper had said. It was when he first told us about the trip, when we knew we were going but hadn't had the final instructions yet. He had mentioned something about Sector 22. Had he meant anything specific by that? Or had he just been talking?

"Is there anything special about Sector 22?" I asked.

Waver pulled out the chart with 22 on it. "Odd you should ask," he said. "I was going to mention 22. It's one of the least explored sectors in the galaxy; a lot of it seems to be incompletely charted. There's no really civilized planet in it, or even near it. Which must be why it's been so neglected. But I did read some interesting reports. Caper's been there, by the way. And there do seem to be some possible planets."

"But it's so far away," Bisty complained.

We talked about it, realizing that it was a long way from our own Sector 9, probably farther than the committee had planned for us to go. Yet they were also the ones who had decided what we were to do, and they must have known what our problems would be. The more we studied the situation, the more Sector 22 seemed to be the answer. Before the evening was over, Gloust and Waver were commissioned to make an intensive study of all they could find out about 22, on charts and in the reports Waver had been reading.

From that day on, we spent almost no time on our

regular classwork. There were only four days left of the octave, and it seemed more important to be ready to go by the end of the pause than to satisfy a meaningless schedule of classes. And for a wonder, none of the teachers complained. Actually the work we were doing took us far beyond anything any of our classes would be studying.

In my own area—ship maintenance and operation—I had succeeded beyond my greatest hopes. I had thought a set of plans might not be easy to come by; but to my surprise, a set of plans for the Q101 just seemed to be there in my basic ship-repair class. I asked if I could borrow them, and everyone seemed to think it would be all right. So I set about all but memorizing them. We would not be allowed to take such detailed plans along, of course. They weren't on the list. So I wanted to have as many details of the ship's construction and capabilities in my mind as possible.

I was pleased with what I found. The ship's landing devices were the best I had ever studied. There was a gamma-ray scope and extra gravitational detection devices, in addition to the usual navigational telescopes. There were good shields for a number of emergencies, all of which could be put into action from under the helmet or manually at the chart desk. In other words, in a real emergency, Caper, who would not be helmeted, could work the emergency equipment. The drive at both helmet and gravity speeds was effective and easy to operate, much like the drives we were used to.

I tried to acquaint the others with the general operations as much as I could. But I didn't burden them with too much of the repair information. I did resolve to take along some tools that I wasn't sure were in the general plan for our trip, but that no one with any sense would go without.

Bisty went about getting the necessary life-support equipment, with a few of the things she wanted to test thrown in. She said that Foker Wand, himself, gave her some tips on just what we might need. It didn't seem quite legal, but Bisty took the advice anyway, and I began to think she might make us comfortable on an asteroid. She also worked on the basic food list, but we all gave her some advice on that.

We shared our knowledge and plans only with each other. The committee members did not come near us. We were not even sure who they were. And we didn't think we ought to ask for advice. Caper had told us that he was our only legal mentor.

Still, as the days went by, the items and information we most wanted always seemed incredibly easy to secure. Someone had to be helping. But even this fed the anger I sometimes felt. It made me sure the staff knew what a difficult thing they had asked of us. And the more I studied for the trip, the more I began to feel that they were expecting too much. We did not talk about this, we four. But I knew that the others, like me, were beginning to be a bit apprehensive.

Our friends asked about the trip and our plans, and we told them as much as we thought was practical, which was almost nothing. They still envied us, and we let them, because although we were coming to see our problems more clearly, we knew that nothing would persuade us to give up the trip, even if we could.

The last three days before we were to go were pause days. Even though we hadn't been going to classes, we were glad of the pause because it took the others off on the usual pause entertainments and out of our way. We worked frantically. I put together the tools I wanted. Bisty worked out the final lists of food we should take. Most of it came packaged in such a way that it could be stretched over a couple of extra days, if necessary. And if we didn't need it all at first, it would keep and could be used later.

She had help on her food list not only from us but also from Quest Wenter, the head of Food Service for the base. I had the feeling that Life Support was determined not to lose Bisty because of bad planning in that department at any rate. She came back from her meeting with Quest Wenter laughing. The tentative list she had made had more than met the demands of the committee. In fact, we had been too frugal.

"Quest Wenter wanted me to put in a bunch of those dessert energy-bars," she said. "Can you imagine wasting space on those?"

Gloust gave her a nasty look. "Sensible man," he said. We all laughed, because we knew how much he liked them. But then, we all did. We had them often, and they were always good.

"Well, you're not getting as many as they wanted me to take," Bisty announced. "There isn't room."

And that took care of that. The supplies that Bisty did want would be delivered directly to the ship's loading dock just before we were to go.

Waver and Gloust moved like comets to duplicate a chart of Sector 22 that Waver had managed to borrow from Reesta Greet. Again, there had been no problem about getting it. Waver said she had seemed a little suprised at our wanting it, but had let him have it without question. Since our allowed equipment didn't include a large, complete chart of Sector 22, we were making a copy to hide aboard the ship.

This was another instance in which we were doing what we felt we had to do, what common sense required. If Sector 22 was the obvious place for us to go, then we had to be prepared to go there. Our final chart of 22 was even more complete than the one Waver had borrowed, because he had added information he had turned up in the old reports he had read.

Waver was really excited about some of the things he had found. "Listen," he said, over and over again. "I think we're on to something, going to 22. There's something funny about that sector. Not only that dark place—"

"Listen yourself," I said. "We aren't going to any dark places. Not if I can help it. You don't know what's there, and neither does anyone else."

"O for the wisdom of a mechanic," he said. "Don't you think I know that? I avoid accretion disks, too. And supernovas when I see them. What I'm trying to say is that there are lots of planets in 22 that have been seen and sometimes even landed on but never put on the charts. They seem never to have been explored—it's as if they're being deliberately hidden. As if someone doesn't want them to be found."

"Nonsense," I said. "They're probably dangerous. That's why they haven't been explored."

"It doesn't sound that way in the records. In fact,

41

there has even been self-space-placement in some of the relatively unexplored areas of 22, and you know they don't allow that unless it's pretty safe."

"Or too dangerous to send a ship," I snapped.

"These people came back," he snorted.

"Did they land anywhere? Report anything concrete?" I pressed. "Or did they just go to a point in space?"

"They didn't land," he had to admit. "But you know you can't carry enough equipment to do any exploring, if you don't have a ship. Don't be so dense, Rom."

I remained unconvinced. "Then why didn't they have a ship, if the area has so much potential?"

Waver just glared at me.

We didn't often quarrel like that. But all of our nerves were a little gone. We'd been working hard. And maybe we were even more worried about the trip than we admitted.

"Look, you two, knock it off," said Gloust. "We don't have time to argue."

"We're all too tense," said Waver. "Let's decide on a course and then take a free day. It will do us good. Let's have a picnic. We need a rest, or we'll really blow it."

He was right. We had become so tight we might not even work well together under the helmets. So we settled down and plotted a course, a good safe course that no one could quarrel with, to a spot in Sector 22 near some of the planets Waver had read reports about. We would move to our spot, hover still, use our detection equipment, and see what was around.

"I wish there was an inhabited planet a little nearer that spot," said Bisty.

"Why?" said Gloust. "It's uninhabited ones we're supposed to be looking for. And besides, not all inhabited planets are safe for us. Inhabited is no guarantee of help in an emergency."

That was true, though not comforting. Some minded species do live on planets that are completely unsafe for us. But it would have been nice if Earth had had at least a few colonies scattered around on livable planets, so we wouldn't feel quite so alone out there. I could feel alone just looking at the chart of 22, so I knew how Bisty felt. But I didn't say anything. No point in stirring up another argument.

Before we went on our picnic, we checked over all the permitted and the secret supplies we had amassed. The next day we would be allowed to board the ship, load our gear, and check things out. Caper would be home sometime during the day, too. And the next day after that, we would be given final instructions, and then we could leave whenever we were ready.

I pointed out on the ship's plan the places where we could hide the extra charts, the tools I was taking, the few extra things Bisty had decided were necessary—water filters and that kind of thing—and some ground probes and other elementary digging tools that Gloust had decided we might need. Probably if we had asked, we would have been allowed to take all of the things we were at such pains to hide. But we didn't want to risk asking. We knew what we felt we had to have, and we didn't want anything to be forbidden.

As ready to go as we could be, we got a packed lunch from the School/Home kitchen and walked to one of the further caves, set up for recreation purposes. This one had what was called artificial grass on the floor, and all the walls reflected a scene of what on Earth was called a park. There were even some artificial trees in the middle. It was very pleasant.

The next day went better than I had expected. The Head of the School/Home, himself, showed us over the ship when we saw it for the first time. He seemed proud of it. And he had a right to be. There weren't many Q101s available yet, and he had been either very lucky or very smart to get one for the School. We sensed when we talked to him that he, for one, wanted us to succeed.

He did not ask us what our plans were, and we hadn't expected him to. He knew that we were to be completely on our own, except for Caper. It must have been a nervous moment for him, turning that beauty of a ship over to four untried kids. Kids that were thought to be daredevils. Yet he never showed it.

We all loved the ship, but I was the most excited. After studying the plans, I had been able to picture just how it ought to look; but to actually see it, and more than that, to know that I was one of four who would be under those helmets was the most exciting thing that had ever happened to me. The ship was so cleverly fitted out, I couldn't get over the wonder of it. There was no wasted space, and the arrangement was such that there could be privacy and comfort for as many as six. We would each have a private berth area. The sanitary facilities were more than adequate and quite self-sustaining. The food storage area was all that Bisty could wish. And I knew we would find it smooth and convenient to operate. In short, it was a great ship.

It stood at a normal dock, the huge doors above closed now, though they would open when we were ready to leave. Around were several of the training ships we were accustomed to using, also standing ready. This was not the main dock area, but the one for the School; yet it was one of the most spacious rooms in the entire underground complex. Behind the docking area were storerooms for gear, and it was here we had piled our carefully collected allowables. Settling them onto the ship was easily accomplished. Once that was done, we brought the items we were less sure of from our pod, carefully concealed, and I soon had them hidden in the places I had chosen.

The food arrived. Bisty counted it out. And grunted when she found a large supply of dessert energy-bars. She stowed everything else away in the ship, then put a few of the bars aboard. The rest she eventually returned to the central storeroom, minus a few that Gloust had taken.

"You have to keep them in your own space," Bisty warned him.

But we all knew that was no problem. They might be gone before we left.

We were almost finished stowing things away when we heard voices outside and discovered that some of our friends had wandered over to look at the ship. We couldn't let any of them come aboard. Everything was so carefully stored and there was so little room for movement, we simply didn't dare. We couldn't risk some damage being done. But fortunately no one seemed to expect to be invited in.

There were even some teachers who had come. We wondered if any of them were committee members, and if so, if they were worried about the future of the ship. Were they afraid that if something happened, people would think it was their fault? They were the ones who had made up this mission, after all. And they should feel responsible for its outcome. Yet, glancing around, we didn't see anyone who seemed worried or upset. Which made me wonder. Had we overlooked some obvious places nearby that would answer our needs? Or were the dangers of deep space overemphasized in some of our classes, so that we wouldn't be too ambitious too soon? Was Sector 22 really quite safe? Waver and Gloust thought so. And I wanted to. But would Caper? Yet he was the one who had first mentioned Sector 22, so I decided he might not be too surprised.

"This trip will be great," I told myself. "You'll be on a Q101. What more could you want?"

Surely the trip would be fun! And besides, Caper wouldn't let us do anything too dangerous. I felt sure of that.

5

Caper came home late that day. We didn't see him when he arrived. He had to check in, make reports and so on, and then sleep. It would be hard on him, we knew, to be making another trip so soon, especially when he wasn't used to it anymore. But we guessed he'd make the best of it.

Morning came after a night of restless sleep for me. I had slept because I knew I must. But I had had dreams of black holes, accretion disks, antimatter, and clouds of hot gas. With our equipment, we should be able to avoid all of these. But that didn't stop me from worrying. I knew from past experience, though, that once we were on our way, I would feel better.

Although he said he hadn't, Gloust looked as if he had slept well and was totally nerveless. Waver is always full of nerves and never seems to need sleep. And

Bisty had probably spent her hours of sleep redesigning her helmet locks.

We were dressed and had just about finished our final check of the ship when Caper came in. He looked glad to see us, a little tired, but eager. There was, in fact, a sense of anticipation about him that I wouldn't have expected. After all, travel to unknown territories wasn't new to him. He'd just come back from a trip of exploration. But none of us said anything. We simply took him aboard the ship and showed him his bunk, the space we had left for his personal gear, and the general way we had stowed things aboard. He left us then to get his gear, full of jolly remarks about the joys of mystery excursions.

"What's made him so Discovery-happy?" Gloust asked.

"Well, I wouldn't think it would be our trip," Waver said. "He's really been around. He was everywhere in those reports I read. I never knew before just how much traveling he did. Going out with a bunch of kids can't mean all that much to him!"

"Maybe it's because it is with kids," I said. "He thinks it's going to be different."

"I think he's been as bored as we are for a long time," Bisty said.

"You could be right," Waver agreed. "I've wondered about those depressions he has when he gets back from a trip."

"Then if we're going to give him the excitement he's been missing, he ought to let us do what we want to do and not to try to play the heavy adviser," I murmured.

Gloust grunted. He didn't have much faith in the generosity of teachers, not even Caper.

48

"We may manage to show him a thing or two," Waver said, optimistic as usual. "There's a lot that's unknown in Sector 22."

I knew that. That was what bothered me. "I thought you'd found enough in those reports to make it less unknown," I said.

"Less unknown, sure," Waver said. "But we're still going to be exploring."

That didn't sound as good to me as it obviously did to Waver, but there wasn't time to say so before Caper was back with his gear.

"When do we leave?" he asked, stepping in.

"We're all ready," Gloust said. "Do you want to check over the ship with us?"

Caper settled his gear and followed us around. I pointed out all the emergency equipment and tested it again with him watching. Then we gauged the oxygen, tried out the various sighting and navigation guides and the suit-making equipment.

"You kids have really learned this ship," he said in amazement. "I thought you didn't get on it until yesterday."

"We didn't," I said. "But I got a set of plans from the ship-repair section and checked everything out. No one said we couldn't," I added as he looked at me in a strange way.

"No," he said, rubbing his chin, "but I guess I didn't think you'd be so thorough."

"We had to be," I said. "Our lives depend on it, don't they?"

"Not quite," he answered. "After all, I'll be there."

He laughed then, but he sounded upset. Because we had done such thorough planning? But what had he expected? He surely knew we weren't the daredevils some people thought we were; not when it mattered. And shouldn't he be glad of what we had done? Or was he one of the ones who wanted us to fail?

"Well, what more have you done?" he asked.

"We've made some plans," Waver said quickly. "We want to take off whenever you're ready. And go to this point." He indicated the place we had chosen in Sector 22. "We'll make three stops on the way—a short hop to Junction 6, then on to Junctions 10 and 14."

I held my breath. Caper had given us the clue to 22, at least it had seemed that way; but had I interpreted his comment correctly? Or would he think it was too far?

He simply grinned, shrugged, and said, "Looks good to me."

"Aren't we supposed to have some sort of send-off?" Bisty asked.

We turned to Caper. None of us knew.

"I'll go see what they want us to do," he said. "This is a little earlier than they had planned for you to leave, but I'm sure it will be all right."

"What's wrong with Caper?" I asked.

"Just excited," Gloust said. "We saw that before."

"No," I told him. "He seemed upset about how much we knew."

"But he thought 22 was all right," Waver said.

"And that's just as strange," I said defiantly. "It really is too far for us, and he didn't even ask if we thought we could make it."

"You worry too much, Rom," Gloust told me.

"Maybe he wants to see us fail, like all the rest," Waver muttered.

That was what I had wondered. Was it possible? He had said that we didn't need to know too much because he'd be there. But surely he couldn't give us too much help without the trip being called a failure.

"Maybe we'd better keep some things quiet for a while, just in case," I said. "He may like Sector 22, but he may not like extra supplies."

Bisty nodded, then Waver.

"Until we're in 22, anyway," Gloust said.

"And one more thing," Waver went on. "Caper may like 22, but if there's to be a farewell committee or something, not all of them may. This is a medium-range ship. They may not want us to take it that far. So if one of them asks where we're going first, why don't we just say to Junction 6? It's the truth. And it will make them smile and say, 'See, these kids really aren't all that bright after all. No need to worry about success here.' " He grinned and glanced around.

We all nodded, though Gloust muttered something about doing what we pleased, regardless.

When Caper came back, the Head and Frecka Umberst were just behind him, along with a couple of teachers we didn't know very well.

"Ready to go?" said the Head.

We said yes.

"It's a little early, but that's all right. You can still be gone for three octaves and three full pauses and a day or two more if you need that much time; we won't demand that with the early start you return earlier than previously scheduled. But if you come home late in the third octave, before the pause, we'll remember you left early."

The Head glanced at the others, who smiled. He

looked pleased with himself and with us, and I decided I really liked him. He was more than fair. And I felt that he, at least, would give us credit for whatever we did manage to do.

The others with him shook hands with each of us, wished us a good journey, and I felt that they were being honest. Before they left, they looked around, checking to make sure we didn't have anything that wasn't supposed to be there, I guess, but they didn't make a big point of it.

When they left, with a final word of parting, I turned on the motor that closed the door, and then we five stood inside looking at each other.

"Might as well go," Gloust said. "Signal for the port doors."

We all turned toward the helmets.

"I'm a little tired still," Caper said. "Why don't I take a nap? You can wake me at Junction 6."

He seemed so relaxed and happy, I wondered if we really did need to worry about him. But that was just the point, wasn't it? He was concerned only that we knew too much. It was a puzzle.

"Come on, let's move," Gloust said.

And we did. It took about ten minutes to get into our helmets, equipped with Bisty's new locks. And, as with all helmet locks, we had to have help. In a ship for four, you pair off and each one of a pair helps the other. Although the helmets depend for movement and direction on basic self-space-placement techniques which everyone learns almost as a baby, they are attached to a lot of gear. The gear is designed to keep four people, or however many are running the ship, from placing at

52

their destination individually and to clear shields and nets set up to prevent random travel. In short, the gear pools the power of all the minds under the helmets and takes the whole ship where they all want to go. The trick is learning to work together: to lift together, to follow a route together, descend together, and to let nothing break the pattern that you are setting together.

This is a lot harder than it sounds. We of Earth are not hive creatures, as some minded species are, and unison thought has to be learned.

I often marvel at our ships. They are the product of an incredible and exacting science. For not only does the gear allow use of self-space-placement in concord, in the Q101 it also allows use of gravity power cells for mechanical lift-off and landing, if that should be necessary, and even for short distance hops at gravity speeds. All this could be controlled by the minds in the helmets. I wondered again at being able to do what we were about to do as I fastened the last of Waver's outer clamps. He moved his head slightly to make sure he was comfortable, and then bent over to finish my fastenings.

"All set?" It was Gloust. Inside the helmets, we couldn't hear anyone speak. But we didn't need to. We knew each other's thoughts. And that was another problem. Part of the training in the use of the helmet has to do with masking thoughts you don't want others to know or that might cause disruption. Now, however, we were all too intent on the trip to be concerned about passing on any thoughts.

Our days of intense training paid off, and our exit was as smooth as anything experienced Discoverers could produce. There one minute, and gone the next, with no lingering parts, no mists or shifting sections. We were proud of ourselves.

Junction 6, our first stop, was not far in one of our ships. Of course, if you could travel alone by self-space-placement, you would get to most places almost at once. In a ship it takes longer. I'm not sure anyone knows why. But the ship does have advantages. It gives you protection and allows you to carry food, water, oxygen, and even clothes and bunks and tools as we were doing. Besides, it gets you through those screens and nets put up these days to keep people from just flitting around by self-space-placement.

It took about twenty-five minutes of focusing to get to Junction 6. We had been trained for trips of up to an hour or an hour and fifteen minutes. So it seemed easy.

We pulled into an electronic slip, using our outer guidance mechanisms, and then moved out of our helmets. Getting out was easier than it had been in any helmets we had used before. Bisty's locks really worked.

Caper opened the door to his bunk as we turned around. "Good trip," he said. "Frecka said you were good, but not how good. Not a slip, not a shimmer, nothing out of place."

"So you approve," I said, laughing, but wanting to see what he would say.

An odd look went over his face before he grinned and said, "Why not, when I'm a benefiting passenger? Of course, if I had been under the helmet . . ."

"We might never have gotten here," Waver joked.

We all laughed, and Caper said, "What now? I've forgotten."

"On to 10," Gloust said. "And then to 14 and then Sector 22."

"Can you go on to Junction 10 now?" Caper asked. It seemed almost a challenge.

"Of course," Gloust said.

"And exactly where are we going in 22?"

We moved to the charts.

"This looked like a pretty good area," Waver said.

"I think I've been near there once or twice," Caper murmured. "Those coordinates seem safe. Anything really dangerous is marked, even on as rough a chart as this."

We all knew that. Dangerous areas were printed in red. This area was a nice, cool, safe blue.

"How far can we go before we have to rest?" Waver asked. "We haven't qualified yet for guaranteed stability and endurance."

Caper smiled. "You'll do," he said. "Go on to Junction 10, and we'll see how you feel then."

So that was that. He went back to his bunk. We clamped ourselves in, and after a study of the route, we were off again. Junction 6 was known territory. But Junction 10 was further than we had ever been, at least in a ship we were driving. So for the first time we really felt as if we were moving toward the unknown.

Under the helmet I could sense that we all felt a little apprehensive, even Gloust. We were off on an adventure, and we were glad we had come. But we knew too much of the dangers of space not to realize that none of us could predict what might happen before we returned to the School/Home. Yet, as we moved smoothly on, our anxieties gradually gave way to a tentative confidence. We were The Terrible Four, and we could do anything. If anyone could succeed on this mission, we could. I even decided to ignore my earlier questions about Caper. For one thing, there was too much else to think about.

6

At Junction 10 we were still nerved-up and ready to move. Caper had evidently gone to sleep, because he did not appear at all. So after a brief rest and something to eat, we went on to Junction 14.

As we steadied ourselves into the slip at 14, I discovered, to my surprise, that I was not only tired, I was exhausted. And one look at the others told me that they felt the same. None of us had ever done three jumps in a row like that, and the last two were long ones.

Caper came out of his bunk before we even got out from under our helmets. He saw how tired we were and looked bewildered.

"We're at 14," Waver said.

Caper said nothing, just went to a viewport. "A long time since I've been here," he murmured. "Not much doing around this junction these days. Used to be on the direct route to a couple of mining planets in 20 from both Upper 15 and Lower 17. But that mining's about done now."

We all dragged ourselves to a viewport and looked out. We were the only ship in the place. There seemed to be no tender ship, even. Big ports generally keep a crew around for emergencies. But there was none here—no installations at all. Only the electronic docks, maintained by one gravity unit.

"Strange there's no one at all here," Gloust said. "It seems to be on a lot of clear routes, and it has plenty of slips."

"Like the ruins of a lost civilization," said Caper. "Ever been to one of those planets? No, of course not. Anyway, all kinds of installations, and no one there. Spooky. But someone must come here from time to time to keep the slips intact, check out the unit. I suppose it's used just for emergencies now. Well, it will serve us for as long as we need it. How long do you plan to stay?"

There seemed to be a challenge in his words. As if he dared us to go on right then.

"I'm too tired to move even myself, right now," I said. I didn't care if he thought I wasn't meeting the challenge. I needed a rest before we went into the real unknown. But I was doing him an injustice.

"You four do need a rest," he said. "You'd be fools to go on. I forget how young you are sometimes. But I don't forget your capacities. Go take a rest, and I'll watch. I'm slept out for now, and with no tender here, someone should stay awake. I've got some book cards I can read if I get bored. Good hot adventure stuff."

We all laughed.

We ate, then slept for eight hours, all four of us. And woke up hungry again.

"Don't eat too much," Bisty said. "Four days this has to last, remember."

"But we've only had a little of it," Gloust muttered. "No point in starving before we need to."

We all laughed. Gloust's appetite was famous.

"Think of this as an adventure into a new dimension, old boy," Waver said. "Imagine yourself as a creature of light, needing only pure energy in small packets to sustain you."

Gloust glowered at him. "Packets of energy, nonsense! Bisty wouldn't even take any dessert energy-bars!"

"We needed the space for protein cubes and vegetable concentrate. Much better for you," Bisty said.

Caper grinned. "I think I may have something in my pack that will tide you over for today, Gloust. But do you really have no dessert energy-bars?" He knew Gloust as well as we did.

"Gloust had some," Bisty said. "And I packed a few in here someplace."

Caper looked thoughtful, even solemn, but I couldn't think of dessert energy-bars as important.

"What about the log?" I asked. "Aren't we supposed to keep an accurate account of what we do?"

All the others had forgotten that.

"Did anyone bring a tape machine?" Bisty asked. "I didn't consider one a part of survival gear."

"Tape is no problem," I said smugly. "The ship has a built-in log. But we have to decide who's going to authenticate it every day. It keeps track of distances and directions in general, and it registers time, but someone has to talk into it to give the specifics."

Even Caper was surprised at that. Evidently he had never shipped out on a Q101. I knew I had told the others about the automatic log, but they'd been so busy with their own work, they hadn't taken it in.

"You do it, Rom," Waver said. "You're best with machines like that."

"If you all want me to," I said briskly. It really wasn't a mechanical problem, but I liked the idea of keeping the log. However, I didn't want to seem too anxious. "I thought maybe we could divide it up. Take turns so they'll know we all went everywhere."

"No one will be that fussy," Gloust argued. "Where is it?"

"Up near the seats."

It was clever equipment, tied in with the navithought guidance system. I showed the others how it was used, and quickly dictated into it the exact course we had taken and other details of what we had done.

"You know," said Caper, when I had finished, "I've been on every kind of ship imaginable, but I've never seen one of those before. Is it permanent, Rom, does it stay with the ship, or are there tapes that come out?"

"It's a permanent part of the ship. There's a device for correcting errors, but basically what's there stays there. A duplicate record of any trip log can be made with some extra equipment we don't have. I suppose they have it at the School/Home so the log of our trip can be studied if someone wants to do it."

"Clever," Caper said, but there was a note of worry in his voice. Did he not want something known about this trip? But that was silly! Besides, if he should want us to fail, which I was beginning to doubt, the log would show our mistakes quicker than anything else.

"Is it on to 22 now?" he asked, changing the subject.

"Why not?" said Waver. "These are the coordinates for the spot we picked. It seems to be the center of the most interesting part of the sector. Even if there should be no planets near, there are some unusual stars and some odd energy sources. It might be worth something to check them out. But I think we'll find planets. My research seemed to indicate we would."

"Just how much research did you do?" Caper almost demanded.

"As much as I had time for," Waver said calmly. "I went through a lot of old Discovery records for 22. There's no point in not knowing all you can before you go."

Once more Caper seemed upset when there was no reason for him to be. We had done a good job of preparing for the trip. Why should that bother him? It was only a passing flick of a look that showed his feelings, however, because he smiled almost right away and said "Good trip" as we turned to get under the helmets.

"What's the matter with him?" Waver asked as we clamped in.

"I don't know," I answered, puzzled. "But he certainly is upset by what we've done. He seems to have expected us to make no plans at all on our own. But he was gone, and we had to do what we could for ourselves."

We both turned to the job at hand, picking out a route, but neither of us was satisfied. Something was wrong, and we didn't know what it was.

The distance we had to cover was actually a little

more than an hour and fifteen minutes. And in spite of our sleep, probably because we had already come so far, we were exhausted when we arrived. My body felt like dead weight.

We sat slumped in our seats, not even moving to pull off our helmets. And we had barely stopped when we were aware of the difference between resting at a junction, even an unused one, and a point in space. There was movement and something more.

"Put the shields up," Gloust thought in a foggy sort of way. It came through to all of us, but it was Caper who did it, with the manual controls. He hadn't heard Gloust, but had felt the need.

I slowly pulled off my helmet and saw the others doing the same. Caper looked at us with concern.

"It was too much for you," he said. "That last jump, with all you'd done before. I should have known. We'll have to rest here awhile. I'll hold the ship steady while you get some sleep. It might take two of you to hold it, but I think I can do it alone."

We all nodded, and with no reply moved off to our bunks. My last thought was that we were going to sleep away our oxygen supply. None of us had thought about that. The food didn't worry me. Even if we got hungry, we could stretch our rations. But we couldn't stretch six days' worth of oxygen. How long would it take to find a planet that would have the atmosphere we needed for resupply?

When I awoke, I got up and went to the ship's log to do what had to be done there. Then I looked around to see who was up and what was going on. Caper was still under the helmet, but he looked tired. The others were nowhere to be seen.

I cut back the shield a small amount and opened a port so I could look out. Black, with a few stars. Nothing near from that view, not that I had expected anything. I turned to the area scanners—which would give a full view all around—the planet analyzer, the gravity testers, and all the other devices. They shared a panel on one wall, at right angles with the helmet seats. I understood the viewing equipment better than anyone else on board, even Caper—he was a plant person, not a mechanic. But Gloust and Waver could both interpret any data I got from the machines better than I.

Remembering my fears just before I went to sleep, I looked for a planet with oxygen first, cursing our ship because it carried no algae to use up carbon dioxide and make oxygen. It seemed odd to me that the School/Home would send us off on a trip of this length in a ship obviously not designed for it. Still, I loved the Q101 and could not fault it in any other way.

The question remained, however—why this ship for this trip? Probably the committee had not intended that we come so far. But why the basic design of the trip then? It almost demanded that we come here, or some place equally distant. All sparsely settled sectors were a long way from the School/Home.

It was too much of a puzzle. Turning back to the panel, I began to take readings. What I needed was the right kind of yellow star. I wished I had the chart that Waver and Gloust had made. Maybe if the others got up and Caper went to bed, we could take it out and use it. In the meantime, I did what I could.

Eventually I found three yellow suns within fairly easy jumps. The gravitational data for all three seemed a good bit alike, but I didn't have enough experience in interpretation to know if it meant possible planets or not. The others were up and putting some food out as I made notes of the data I had gotten and did a rough estimate of where the yellow stars were.

Caper ate with us, remaining under the helmet. Then Bisty and I clamped in and explained to him that we thought he should take a nap while we held the ship and Waver and Gloust tried to find a good planet, based on my data and the charts.

"I wish we had better charts," Caper said. For the first time he seemed really anxious. "I've been trying to remember what I've seen in this area, but it's hard to think under the helmet and do your job, too."

We agreed.

"It's nice of you to try, anyway," I said. "But after all, we're the ones who are supposed to do the finding. Waver is awfully good on the mathematics of these things. He'll know if there are any planets near."

Caper gave me an appraising look, then went off, stopping first to examine the data I had collected and to take a quick look at the outspread charts.

The minute he was gone, Gloust and Waver brought out the hidden chart. They began some work with my data on the computer, and then turned to the big sector chart.

Finally Gloust came over to the helmets and got under one. I clamped him in, and he told me to go out and help Waver. They needed more information.

I went to the chart desk, and Waver pointed out the area he needed explored. Turning the scanner in that direction, I realized he was interested in one of the yellow suns I had located earlier, the farthest away, a

60/40 bearing from the ship's coordinate, in a rising manner.

I got the information Waver needed, and after a hasty computer runout, he decided that the star had planets.

Quickly we plotted a course to the star. A twelve-minute jump would put us near enough to see what we had. We decided to go while Caper was asleep so we could all watch the chart.

Under the helmet, before we left, Waver passed me a brief thought while Gloust and Bisty were clamping in. He was still worried about Caper. "He wants something from this trip," he said. "Something that may or may not have anything to do with us. He doesn't mean us harm, I'm sure. But I think he has something in mind that was not in the original plan." It sounded crazy. But Waver has an odd sensitivity to people. And he was often right when he made wild guesses like that. So I didn't just dismiss what he said. But I wasn't sure I agreed.

I had no time to think about it though. We were ready to go. Our destination was an observation point that would let us see planets, if there were any. It was a somewhat shorter trip than I had thought it would be—ten minutes. But local conditions sometimes make a difference in time—something to do with gravity.

Once stopped, I snapped out of my helmet and dashed over to the scanners, while Gloust put the chart away. Waver and Bisty held the ship.

There were planets! I could have screamed with relief. Five of them. More than I had hoped for. The two inner planets would be impossible: too hot. But the third might work. I turned on the planet classifier and beamed it at the third planet. The readout showed an atmosphere, thin, but with oxygen.

I turned as soon as I had the data recorded and handed it to Gloust, who stood behind me.

"One problem," I said. "It has a lot of gravity. It won't be an easy planet to pull away from."

"And less chance of available water and life," Gloust said.

I hadn't thought of that. "There are two planets I haven't tested. I can try them, but this is in the best position for what we want."

He nodded, and I ran a check on the other two. Not as promising. So we decided we had better take a chance on what we had.

We all four got under the helmet to consult. "It's oxygen that's the real worry," Bisty said. "I knew it would be. Then water. I think we'd better try it."

We were studying the coordinates when Caper came out, and we did not stop to explain, but simply took off. In three minutes we were close enough to get a good look. In fact, we could even see the planet in the viewport. I unclamped to get a look in the scanners. The gravity was heavy, as I had thought. No life. I was almost certain of that. But close up, the scanner showed quite a bit of oxygen.

To Caper, who seemed amazed at finding himself where he was, I explained briefly. He looked over my data with more attention than I thought was really necessary. "Well, shall we set down?" I asked finally.

"Takeoff will be harder than you're used to," he offered. I knew that. "But I'm sure you can do it. And we'll all feel better with an oxygen renewal. We'd better

66

not get out of the ship, though. I don't like everything I see in that atmosphere."

I nodded and got back under the helmet. We set out and landed the ship as gently as we could. It seemed odd for a planet that size and in that place to have so much gravity. But I tended to think of all planets about that distance from a star as being like Earth, although of course they're not.

Once down, Bisty turned on the oxygen renewers, and we were all glad to see the reservoir index move up. While the renewer was at work, we ate again, checked the charts, and I showed Caper the other two stars that might have planets.

"You're right," he said. "Before we try something farther away, I think we should have a look at those."

Once we'd eaten, since none of us were needed to hold the ship, we went to bed. When we got up six hours later, Waver and Gloust worked out the coordinates for a safe place near the next star, I did the log, and Bisty checked the water, then the food. She doled some out, then said, "We have to be careful. Eat less. And that means you, too, Gloust."

"Have to keep up my strength," he said, grinning. "Monsters might attack on one of these planets. And I'm the only one with defense training."

We all laughed.

"Don't show your muscles too soon," Waver advised. "They might scare the monster away. And even monsters might be good to eat, if we're hungry enough."

I laughed again and turned back to the log. It kept track of the time in School/Home hours, and showed that we had been gone just about two days. It seemed a lot longer. I wondered if we had eaten just two-day's food supply. We had started out with only enough for four days. We were going to need a planet with food soon.

"Can we count this as one planet?" I asked, suddenly remembering what we were supposed to be doing.

Caper looked up surprised. "I'd almost forgotten what we were out here for. Yes, you can count this as one, if you need it."

If we needed it? What did that mean? Well, maybe that we'd have to visit a lot more than three planets to find all of the things we needed to survive.

At last the oxygen tanks were full—a whole six days' worth. Bisty turned off the renewer, and we all stood around the chart desk, absorbing the route to the star we had chosen.

"Do you want me to get under the helmet for the takeoff?" Caper asked.

"This is our trip," Gloust said. "We have to do it ourselves."

"Good old Gloust," quipped Waver. "Ever willing to wear us out with hard labor. But you're right. We have to keep this trip honest."

Bisty and I agreed. We might need to use Caper under the helmet sometime when we were moving. But not yet. It was our trip, and as long as possible, the log ought to show that we four had run the ship. Holding it in place from time to time was something else.

Yet taking off was not easy. For a second, I wondered if we would make it on our own or if we should use the gravity drive as well. But I hated to suggest it. We might have greater need for our power cells later. If Caper was right and we had to visit a lot of planets before we found food and water, we didn't dare waste anything.

7

We simply hung in the sky above the new sun, tired again. It was just an eight-minute trip from the last planet, but the effort of lift-off had worn us out. I had expected problems on this expedition, but none of the problems I had worried about had been labeled exhaustion. In fact, I didn't know why we were so tired. The energy drain we were subject to in driving the ship was part of it, but that didn't seem the whole answer.

We needed rest again, but we also needed to find food and water. So after a brief nap and a snack, I checked out the sun for planets, found it had four, and we decided that the second of the four looked best. We landed, but it was a disappointment. No sign of life anywhere.

"One thing you have to say," Bisty announced as we gazed at the barren mess out of the viewports, "unless we find something a lot different from anything we've seen, we aren't going to have to worry about Gloust's monsters."

Caper laughed and said, "I could have told you that monsters were unlikely."

"That depends on your definition of a monster," Gloust said.

There was nothing to do then but try the last of the three suns I had originally found. I plotted the coordinates while the others pored over the School/Home chart for other possibilities.

Waver wanted me to check out a star in the middle of a large dark area that had intrigued him ever since he and Gloust had made up the chart of 22. Waver is always interested in the mysterious. But Gloust said a prompt no. And I seconded him. Neither of us wanted to explore a place that might hold unseen dangers.

While the three of us were arguing over the star, Bisty was checking the food. She announced that there was not as much left as she had hoped.

Helmets on again, we moved toward the third sun. We were sluggish, and the trip took longer than it should have. I didn't understand it. Only Gloust seemed to have any semblance of his usual energy. I could only think it was because he was bigger than the rest of us.

When we arrived at the new coordinates, the others stayed under the helmet while I moved to the scanners. I was beginning to feel desperate, and hoped that this time I would find something just right. It was a yellow star. We had known that. But I found no evidence of planets, though the gravity scan had been about the same as it was for the others, which had had planets.

Why? A quick further check frightened me almost out of my skin. The star had a dark companion! This was no place to stay.

We decided to go immediately to the place in 22 where we had started out. By the time we arrived, we were once again exhausted. Caper looked tired, too, but he motioned us to our bunks and put himself under a helmet to hold us. I worried about him out there alone. What would happen if he slept and didn't hold us steady?

My mind tried to cope with the problems we would have if we should drift. The log would help us know how far we had gone and in what direction, but it would not be accurate enough for us to know exactly where we were. Only by sighting known stars, preferably the ones used for basic navigation, and figuring from the angles and true relations of three or more of them could we be sure of our position. And that would take time. Worrying about this kept me awake for at least three minutes after I fell into my bunk.

The next thing I knew, Gloust was knocking at my door. I heard him call my name and tried to ignore him. It couldn't be time to get up already!

"Rom!" Gloust sounded desperate.

I forced my eyes open and sat up, at least as far as the bunk would permit. There was more movement of the ship than there had been before I went to sleep. But we couldn't have taken off. Besides, helmet drive gave no feeling of motion if it was done well.

"Romula!" It was almost a scream. And this time it was Waver.

I hadn't bothered to undress when I lay down, so I

opened the door and hurried out. Both Gloust and Waver were there.

"Caper is asleep," Gloust said. "I woke up and felt the movement. We're drifting."

It didn't sink in for a moment. I had thought about it, but I had never imagined it would happen.

"How long?" I asked finally.

"Don't know," Gloust said. "We only slept about two hours. Bisty is trying to hold us, wherever we are. You're the one who knows the guidance equipment best. You've got to do something."

Had my thinking of it made it happen? No, that was ridiculous; it was because Caper had looked so tired that I had thought of it. I hurried toward the log. I wasn't quite sure how to get information from it, but discovered that there were directions inside the cover, and I hastily noted down the distance and direction of drift.

"Get out your chart," I said. "We can't care now if Caper wakes up and sees it."

At the scanners, I probed the sky. What big stars were near? This part of the galaxy had fewer beacon stars than most others. Then suddenly I remembered Waver's dark area, and the star in the middle. Yes, there it was on the chart. Could I find it in the sky? That would give me an approximate location. Most of all it would help me identify other stars. But only if we stayed still ourselves!

"Gloust, we're not steady yet," I called. "Bisty can't do it alone. And Caper is still sleeping." How could he sleep, I wondered, with so much going on around him?

Gloust quickly got under a helmet, and the ship settled. That made my job easier. I scanned the sky for a large dark area. I swept the sky again and again. And then at last I got a pattern that seemed right. Black, with a center star. It seemed to match the chart. And I gave Waver some coordinates to check.

It was another hour, however, before we had firmly established our position. We had not drifted far. Just enough to make our surroundings look different and to throw off any calculations we might have made. I glanced down at the notes I had been making. I had done readouts on at least a dozen stars. Were there any among them that might have planets? One or two were yellow, but none with enough indication in their motion to be sure. I handed their coordinates to Waver, however, who checked them on the big chart of 22. No indication there, either, of planets. But we had to find something, or our food and water would give out.

"What's the closest star on the chart that shows planets?" I asked finally. We had to find a place to rest, if nothing else.

"Half hour," Waver said.

"We'd better go there. To rest and sleep, if nothing else."

Waver nodded. "What about Caper?"

"Put him in his bunk." I said.

We couldn't manage that, however. He was too heavy—absolutely dead weight. But his pulse felt all right. I couldn't imagine what was wrong with him. We pulled him from under the helmet and stretched him out on the floor.

"He'll be all right there," Waver said. "Good night, sweet prince. We angels shall flight thee to a firmer rest."

I laughed. Even in an emergency, Waver had a quote.

"Shakespeare. Pre–Clordian Earth poet. Way back," Waver muttered as we fastened each other into helmets. "And that's not exactly what he said."

"Somehow, I didn't think it was," I said, laughing, glad Waver had made a joke, because our situation was not something we could laugh over. Soon we would be desperate. The new planets simply had to have something to offer. The sun was a nice one, and its third and fourth planets did seem possible. The smaller of the two was the more likely. I worked the machines, then beckoned to Gloust, who got out from under his helmet to take a look.

"How's this?" I asked. "Do you think it might do?"

"It's pretty small," he said. "But you're right. There's almost sure to be water. And there does seem to be free oxygen in the atmosphere. There might not be useful vegetation. But water will at least help."

"And sleep," I said. "That last was barely a nap. There'll be gravity to hold us anyway."

"OK, let's go," he said.

We headed in, but because the configurations of the planet were not clear, we moved to a spot above the surface and guided the ship in under gravity drive, using a viewport and the telescreen.

"It's green," Bisty said.

And it was. Big green. The vegetation—or whatever it was—looked lush. It was hard to know what would happen if we set the ship down in the middle of it. So we moved gently above the surface until we found a rocky outcrop. It was a rough landing because the rocks were uneven, but when the telescreen showed us a little of the density and height of the vegetation below, we were glad of what we had done.

"Sleep!" said Waver, pulling off his helmet.

It was the only thing anyone said. We all hurried to our bunks. But before I went to sleep, I tore a piece of paper out of a chart pad and left a note for Caper in case he should wake up. I hoped there was nothing wrong with him. It seemed odd that he should sleep so long and so soundly.

I was glad the log recorded time, because I had lost all track of it. That was my first thought when I woke. I wondered if regular Discoverers felt that way or if they developed some inner time sense. I'd have to ask Caper. Which made me wonder if he was still sleeping. I got up to see.

The others were not up. And neither was Caper. He was still on the floor. So I decided to straighten things up a little, mostly to take my mind off my empty stomach. The ship was so messy, it was hard to find anything. I made order out of the charts, put the large 22 chart away, and swept crumbs of protein cubes and vitamin wafers from the floor. The larger of them I ate.

Near the seat where Caper had slept under the helmet, I found an odd capsule: nothing I remembered our bringing along. Some kind of drug, I thought, opening it and sniffing. And then I did remember. It was like the capsules Caper took sometimes when his leg hurt. The capsules blocked the pain and generally put him to sleep. Had he taken one—or more? Was that his problem? Would he do that sitting under the helmet? Responsible for holding the ship! The idea horrified me. Had he deliberately put himself to sleep? Didn't he value his own safety, if ours didn't matter to him?

76

I put the two parts of the capsule back together and slipped it into the pocket of my shirt. I didn't know for sure what I would do with it. But I was going to keep it.

Waver came out as I stood there, still puzzling over what I had found. He looked around appreciatively. "Our little housekeeper," he said. "I thought you were the machine expert, but obviously you have other talents. Have you cooked breakfast, too?"

"A many-faceted genius," I said. "But not one that can create food out of nothing. In fact, one that is about to die of starvation if that green stuff out there can't be eaten."

"Well, I pledge this: You will not starve alone." He stood beside me at the viewport. "There's so much of it. Surely some of it ought to be useful. And there must be water."

I showed him the capsule then, and told him where I had found it. He was as horrified as I had been.

"Don't tell the others," he said, after cursing Caper roundly. "We may be wrong. And besides, this is his third trip with almost no rest in between. And his leg may have really hurt."

"You don't think he did it on purpose?" I asked.

"Well, he obviously took the capsule. Or it certainly looks as if he did. But maybe he didn't think he would go to sleep. I don't think he would deliberately put us all in danger. Why would he?"

I didn't know. And there were too many other things to worry about to spend time on a question we couldn't answer. "What next?" I asked.

"Take a look at the chart to see what's near if this one doesn't work," Waver said.

While he checked the charts, I went to the scanners to see what I could pick up. I didn't get much. And before I finished, Gloust and Bisty appeared, and then finally Caper woke up.

"Where are we?" Caper asked, confused.

"On one of the planets of, as far as we know, an unnamed star in Sector 22," Waver told him.

"How long did I sleep?" Caper asked. Then, as if it were a new and awful thought, he said, "Did I go to sleep under the helmet?"

We all nodded.

"For how long?"

"We don't know exactly," I said, "but it was less than two hours before we discovered it. We were about thirty seconds away from our hold position. But I don't know what forces were moving us and how fast."

Caper looked amazed and, I thought, disappointed. "How far is this?"

"Nearly a half hour."

"How did you find it?"

"Sheer luck!" Waver said quickly. It was almost the truth. "We had to set down and get some real sleep, and this seemed as good a place as any. It's a small planet, but it sure has a lot of growth. Which I hope means water and food."

Caper went to the viewport, looked out, and flinched visibly. It was only then that I remembered that his old injury came from a planet with a very rapid growth.

"Bad stuff, this small planet growth," he said. "But there might be water. What are we sitting on?"

"A rock outcrop," said Gloust. "Is there anything to eat?"

"Not much," said Bisty.

"Then let's hope that stuff out there is edible," Caper said. "I doubt it, but it's possible."

After we ate and drank a little, not nearly enough, it was decided that Caper, Gloust, and Bisty should go exploring. Waver and I would stay aboard in case someone needed rescuing. Bisty ran up some of the general-purpose suits the ship could make—one for each of us. These were designed for planets of unknown structure. When the three left, Caper took the ground explorer with him, planning to dig for water if he had to. They moved carefully out of the air lock, ready for anything outside.

Bisty came back a half hour later. "Caper has found some roots he thinks might be edible, and there's water. Come on out and bring those carrying cases for food and water."

The planet was not what I had expected. It was warm and green, but not really pleasant. The air felt heavy, and I was soon damp all over inside my suit.

Because the gravity was low, moving was easy. The hard thing was to keep from bounding up at each step.

The water was in the earth, but Caper had not had to dig too far to find it. As the hole he made filled up, we dipped in our keep jars. The full jars were heavy, and it took two of us to carry each one. But eventually they were all in the ship, along with a small box of roots. Bisty was going to test them, but Caper said he would do that while she ran a check on the water. He pronounced them edible, and we went back out to gather some more. They might not be the last word in delicious dining, but at least they would keep our stomachs from feeling like great empty caverns.

It was about to grow dark in our area of the planet

when we came back to the ship from our gathering expedition. We ate a few of the roots, along with the last of our regular rations for an evening meal. I didn't eat as many roots as the others, because I thought they tasted terrible. Maybe tomorrow we'd find something better. If not, we had plenty of roots. I could eat them then, when I was more desperate.

We decided to sleep awhile, and after we awoke to decide another destination and take off. This planet might have food, water, and oxygen, but it was too oppressive a place to stay long. The growth was too dark and heavy, and the air too sultry.

"Nobody ever told me that Discovery was three-quarters sleeping," Waver complained as he opened the door to his bunk.

We all laughed, but I was reminded of Caper's sleep. Had he taken those drugs on purpose? And if so, why? There had to be an answer. It was that old worry bug at me again. But it didn't keep me from sleep. Nothing, it seemed, could do that.

We were all up, however, long before we had expected to be. Those roots had not been as edible as Caper had thought. We were all sick. We raced outside and heaved and heaved and heaved. Then we sat down on the floor inside, shaken and weak. It could have been the water or some germ we had picked up, but Caper decided it was the roots. And I tended to agree, since I wasn't as sick as the rest, and I hadn't eaten as many of them. So much for Caper the great plant expert, I thought. But anyone can make a mistake, especially facing starvation.

The worst of it was that our food from the base was

gone. So once we were over being sick and were hungry, there was nothing at all to eat. Bisty tested the water again, and assured us it was safe. So we had water and oxygen. But food was essential, too.

There might have been truly edible plants on that planet, but none of us had the heart to look for them. The only sensible thing to do then was to leave right away, while we still had some energy left. But where to go? My check of other planets around the local star had given nothing positive. So that meant finding another star and, if we were lucky, another set of planets. But where? There was no longer a margin for failure.

I looked at Waver, and he nodded. Time to bring out the chart of 22.

Caper looked a little startled, but said nothing until it lay before us. Then, without commenting on it, he began to search for something.

"As you keep reminding me, I'm not supposed to help," he said. "But you are supposed to survive this trip, and I am too. And you have been to three planets, and you have found supplies of a sort. So let me see if I can find a planet I remember—one I visited once." He pored over the chart, then turned to us. "Here it is. This star has planets, and the third planet is habitable. I'm sure that's the place." He pointed to a star we hadn't even considered.

"You're sure it's all right for us to take your advice?" Waver asked.

"Who's going to know?" Caper asked. "You could have come upon it yourselves."

That was true, in a way. And we were desperate. Besides, it was Caper's fault we were in so much trouble.

His sleeping and his roots. So we agreed to go to his planet.

It was a fifteen minute trip, but looking at the others, I knew it would take longer than that. We'd be lucky to make it at all.

Caper looked around and obviously saw what I saw, all of us pale and listless. "Rom, do you know how to run the food-resource tester?" he asked.

"Of course I do," I snapped. What did he think I was?

He ignored my irritation. "You're in better shape than the rest of us. You didn't eat as many roots. Go lie down on your bunk. I'll take your place under the helmet. Those of us under the helmet will be in no shape for anything when we get there. But you'll have some energy left to go out and get us something to eat."

"But you're the plant expert," I said, with more irony than I had intended.

He winced and said, "I've got more guaranteed endurance than any of you. And we're going to need endurance to get there."

I couldn't quarrel with that, so I went to my bunk and lay down. I didn't sleep, but tried to put together the steps I should take for finding food. I realized that I might also have to guide us to a landing, so I didn't dare actually sleep.

About thirty minutes later, I felt the ship shiver and stop at the coordinate we had set. I hurried out to find the others hardly able to move under the helmets. The third planet, Caper had said. I worked up the coordinates quickly, and guided the others to the spot I had chosen. Then from a hastily opened viewport and from the telescreen, I selected a landing site. The planet seemed to be largely ocean, with a few scattered bits of

82

land. I chose the largest of them. It took only a moment to adjust the controls for gravity power; and with the hand gear, I guided the ship in to what seemed to be an area of growing things and water.

Once I had set the ship on the ground, I helped the others to their bunks, grateful for the ease with which Bisty's helmet locks could be unfastened. The four were asleep almost before they lay down. But food was what they really needed. All I could hope was that what I had seen outside the ship would prove to be edible. If it wasn't, I didn't see how we could survive.

After putting on one of Bisty's all-purpose suits and picking up the portable food tester, I stepped out of the upper air lock, went down the steps and out the bottom air lock. That door I locked from the outside with the emergency key, and left the others locked in behind me.

8

My legs felt shaky as I stepped down to the ground. I didn't know if it was fear or weakness. I hadn't really looked at the planet as I set the ship down, except to note that it was mostly water, and this area looked to be the most habitable. But now as the land spread before me, I could only stand and gaze at it with wonder. And all the tensions and anxieties of the past few days drained out of me. I did not know what dangers there might be or what problems I might face. But in that first moment, what mattered was the beauty. I had grown up seeing pictures of Earth, being surrounded by images of Earth. But nothing had prepared me for stepping into a real Earth-like landscape. Without thinking about what I was doing, I pushed my helmet back. I wanted to feel the air, smell it. I wanted to be a part of everything around me with all my senses. No one had ever told me how sweet a breeze could smell. No one had told me how gently the wind could brush my face, how exciting the movement of a leaf could be. I was transfixed, and for long moments hardly knew that I was I.

Eventually my stomach reminded me that I had a mission to perform. I had to analyze what I had only been enjoying. The ship stood on a flat plain covered with a deep, blue green plant. It looked like pictures I had seen of a plant called grass on Earth, so I called it grass. In one direction—I called it north, based on the direction of the planet's rotation—there was what on Earth would be called a forest, about two kilometers or so away. Large treelike plants rose to end the plain, and in the distance beyond, the land broke into hills that eventually rose into mountains. On either side, to the east and west, the plain and its grasses gradually gave way to Earth-like bushes and then more of the trees that lay to the north. The trees were closer on the west than the east, and there were fewer bushes on the west. To the south the plain widened, the bushes and trees tapered off and finally seemed to disappear.

The air was cool but pleasant. I walked away from the ship, wondering which way to go. The bushes perhaps on the east. I seemed to remember that on earth, bushes sometimes bore fruit that was edible.

Walking slowly across the plain, I was aware of the fact that I had brought no protective weapon of any kind, but I didn't care. I was hungry, and I didn't care much about that either. What mattered most was the miracle of that planet. It was just so beautiful. Lovely plants, bending in the breeze. A warm sun and a cool wind, and a sky that seemed to fill all space with its blue.

Eventually I came to some of the plants I called bushes. They formed a large patch on the bank of a stream of water. Without testing it, I drank. Cold and sharp and good! Then I turned to the bushes. I had begun to feel warm. The sun was rising in the sky, and the day was getting hot. I longed to take off my protective suit, especially since it didn't have air conditioning. But I just opened the fasteners to let a little air in.

The bushes were lovely things. Long branches full of dark green leaves and something else. This was where some of the sweet smell in the air originated, the dark blobs on the branches. I reached over and pulled one off. It was soft and appealing. I tested it quickly, and it seemed all right. Then, not only because I was hungry but even more because I wanted to consume something that belonged to this world, to become, in a way, a part of it, I ate one. Sweet and delicious! I picked another and another. I couldn't stop eating. I ate until I thought I would burst.

Now I'll be sick, I thought. But I sat down on a stone beside the stream to look around and rest, and I felt fine, just fine.

It was hard to remember the others in the ship or to consider possible hazards. Wild beasts might appear. There might be representatives of a dangerous, minded race ready to descend upon me. It didn't matter; I was absorbed in the beauty around me.

Finally, though, I did have to think of the others. They might wake up and be worried. I had brought nothing to collect food in, an oversight neither Bisty nor

Gloust would ever have made. But I simply took my helmet entirely off, closed the face mask, and used the whole thing as a carrier.

It took only a few minutes to fill the helmet with fruit—yes, that was the Earth word, I was sure. *Berries* was what this particular sort of thing might be called. The quantity available argued that there must be few pickers, though much of it, to my untrained eye, did not seem ripe. Many of the berries were hard and green.

I should have been tired as I walked back to the ship, but I felt rested and alert. The air was even warmer now, and I yearned to take off my suit, yet I didn't quite dare to do that. Still, I enjoyed my stroll and quickened my pace only as I came near the ship. Then I could hardly wait to share what I had found with the others.

Even so, I stepped inside the air lock with reluctance. I didn't want to leave the glorious out-of-doors. The inside would be cool and dark and sterile. All my life, it seemed, had been dark and protected and dull. Why had no one ever told me what a habitable planet was like?

Waver was awake, and he must have seen something in my face when I pushed open the upper door.

"It's good," he said, looking at me. A momentary sputter of enthusiasm crossed his limp, tired face.

"Better than anything has ever been," I told him. "You have to come out and see."

"Not until I have some of whatever you have in there. I assume they're edible."

I was impatient with his lack of response. "They test all right. And I ate a whole lot of them. They're good."

Waver frowned. "Bisty will tell you there's no protein in them."

"Oh, bother protein. Look, I'll put some in one of those field carrying-cases while you get into a suit. Let's go out; you can eat there. It's so much nicer than in here."

He looked at me as if I had lost my mind, but I kept at him until he finally agreed.

He took the case with the berries, and I took a handful more for myself. We also took the field food tester and, this time, a laser protector. As we stepped out, Waver still looked as if the whole enterprise was insane. But we had barely had time to lock the lower door and glance around than, looking at him, I knew he understood. He wasn't even eating the fruit, just standing and staring.

"Do you suppose this is the only place in the whole galaxy like this?" he asked finally. "Or do Discoverers find others sometimes?"

"I think Earth must be something like this," I said slowly. "And I think there must be others, too. There are a lot of places that aren't good for us. But I think there must be a lot that we would like. They say that nothing in the galaxy is single. What exists in one place, exists in others. Nobody has really proved that. But everyone assumes it's true. So there have to be other places like this and like Earth. And Discoverers must find them. Maybe even your parents or mine. Though not this one. It isn't on the charts."

"Have you stopped to think about that?" Waver asked, eating the berries now. "Caper knew about it. He knew just where it was. And yet these planets weren't even on that detailed chart. He must have been here with an expedition. Yet no one reported it. Why?"

It was odd. If an expedition had reported the planet, it would have been on the map. Though after a long trip, I supposed, one planet could have been forgotten; it could have been left out of the reports by mistake. But how could anyone forget a place like this? "Maybe no one thought it was important," I said finally.

"Then why did Caper remember it?" Waver persisted.

"Because he loved it," I said.

We looked at each other. Somewhere in all of this lay the answer to the questions we had been asking ever since the trip began. But neither of us could quite put the pieces together. And we didn't even want to just then. Waver grabbed my hand, and we ran, a slow jogging trot, toward the trees in the west, the opposite direction from the one I had gone before.

We came finally upon another stream and flopped down beside it, breathless and laughing. Beyond were some low bushes, a small patch of them, that bore some kind of fruit, and beyond them were the trees. Waver picked one of the fruits and tested it. I sat with my hand on his shoulder, peering over at the results. It was edible. Waver picked another one and ate it, then fed me yet another.

"Not bad," he said. "Not sweet like the first. A tangy taste. Good."

We both set about filling the field carrying-case, picking as many as seemed ripe, to take back to the others, eating occasionally as we worked. Waver filled his helmet, too. I had left mine on the ship.

The planet had rotated a good distance before we

were back at the ship. We had picked slowly, stopped to talk and to admire the place, even sat for a while talking, our backs against a rock. When we finally strolled casually back across the plain, we thought we might see the others out, but there was no sign of their having left the ship.

"I have the only key," I said, remembering suddenly. "They could get out, but they couldn't lock the door behind them. And I don't suppose we ought to go off and leave the ship unlocked. Though we haven't seen anything dangerous. No animals of any kind."

"Which is not good," Waver said. "We need protein. If there are no animals, we'll have to try to find some plants with protein, and that may not be easy."

We opened the air lock and went in. Caper and Bisty and Gloust were sitting in the helmet seats without the helmets on. My outside helmet was in front of them, empty.

"It's about time," Gloust muttered. "You certainly weren't in any hurry to get back."

"But I left the fruit. That was all I'd found until Waver and I came upon these."

We put the new fruits down.

"Is it all right to eat?" Bisty asked.

"Well, we ate it," Waver said. "And it hasn't done anything to us yet."

"But your faces are red," Bisty said. "You look as if there's something wrong with you."

Waver's face did look red. I felt my own, and it felt hot to the touch. But I didn't feel bad.

"I don't know," I said. "My face is hot, but my stomach is all right."

Caper laughed. "Serves you right for leaving us so

long. There's nothing really wrong with you. It's this sun. You're not used to it, and you took your helmets off. You're sunburned, that's all."

"Sunburned," Waver said curiously. "But this is not an inner planet. It's cool outside. Very nice."

Caper laughed again. "What do your planet survival courses teach you? People whose skin is not accustomed to the sun burn the first few times they go out in it, even on a cool planet. Then the skin puts up a protection—it gets dark—and doesn't let so much of the sun penetrate. After that you don't burn as easily. Put your faces against some cool piece of metal here on the ship, and then go into the first-aid kit. I'm sure there's something there for sunburn. It's standard equipment on Discovery trips. It happens all the time. But smart Discoverers don't make a habit of it."

"Does that mean we'll always have to wear a helmet?" I asked. The breeze, and even the sun, on my face had felt so nice.

"No, I'm sure we have some cream aboard that will help you build up protection in your skin. But if we're going out for a whole day, we ought to have some hats. Maybe we can make some that won't be as confining as the helmets, something that will cover the top of the head and shade the face."

Bisty nodded, taking up the challenge, as I went to find a cool piece of metal and then the cream. My face was really beginning to hurt.

Waver and I stayed in, where it was cool and out of the sun, while the others took their turn exploring. We hated it, but Caper said we might be sick if we got more sun right away.

When the others came back, they were as excited as

91

we had been. I had never seen Gloust so enthusiastic.

"Why do people live in places like the School/Home when there are planets like this?" he asked. "It's so free here. So real. Why couldn't the School/Home be here instead of where it is? And why doesn't anyone ever tell you there are places like this?"

"Because Earth does not colonize habitable planets, only unlivable ones," Caper said. And I sensed an anger in his voice. "People stay on Earth or they work as Discoverers or at Discovery bases. The feeling is that not enough people have left Earth to justify our taking over and colonizing a planet like this."

"Is Earth like this?" Bisty asked.

"Something like this, I suppose," Caper said. "I've never been there."

"But it's not fair!" Gloust said. "We don't even have a choice. We can't go to Earth. And they say we can't live on a place like this—only in those underground holes they make for bases. What right do they have to do that to us?"

"They want you to grow up and go out and explore— find the minerals and things Earth needs, help other minded races find what they need. That's Earth's contribution to the general galactic culture. And there are never enough people willing to be Discoverers." Caper seemed disturbed.

"But what if you're not good at Discovery? What if it doesn't seem all that important to you?" Waver asked.

"Oh, they'll find a place for you," Caper said. "You may hate it, but they aren't going to let you wallow in old poets and philosophers, or even in pure math. Once you leave Earth, action is more important than ideas."

"But we didn't leave Earth," Waver said. "So why can't we go where we want to go, be what we want to be?"

There was no answer to that. We were all silent for a moment. Then I asked, "But is this really like Earth? And are there other planets like this?"

"I've seen a few others somewhat like this," Caper said. "And I do think it is like Earth. A primitive Earth; Earth before people."

"I wish we could just stay here," Gloust said. "There seems to be food enough. And I'm sure I could build some kind of shelter."

Caper gave him an appraising look, full of approval. "I don't think the five of us could settle a planet on our own. We're too few, really." But he didn't sound out of sympathy with the idea. In fact, it sounded as if he, too, longed for the freedom and the beauty we had all found so wonderful. I wondered then if love for a place like this was part of our Earth heritage, even if we had never been to Earth itself.

"Where did you learn about shelters?" Caper added after a moment's pause.

"We each learned things that had to do with our specialty," Gloust explained. "I found information on shelter building, along with some other stuff on exploring wild planets."

"Well, this is a wild one all right," Caper said. "Let's let Rom figure out how long we can stay here. It must be something over two octaves and a couple of pauses. That should give us a good taste of outdoor life."

"That's not long enough," Gloust protested.

I turned to the log to begin checking time, but as I

did, I looked at Waver. And I could tell that he was wondering, as I was, if we were on this planet by accident or by someone's design. Yet I didn't care. I loved being there, however it had happened.

9

Both Waver and I had very sore faces the next day, in spite of what the first-aid kit had produced to help us. But we did not intend to be left inside. So with Bisty's help, we managed to devise some brimmed hats that would protect our faces from the sun.

"We'd better all have some," Caper said. "We may be out all day. We should explore the area, decide if we want to stay here or move somewhere else. If we do stay, I think we should move the ship over near those trees, where it won't be quite so obvious. We really don't know that there are no minded species here. And it wouldn't be a good idea to call attention to ourselves."

"If someone is around, wouldn't they have seen us come down?" Gloust asked.

"Yes, but an entry like that goes so fast, watchers think they're mistaken."

It sounded logical.

"Weren't you here before?" Waver asked. "Did it have any minded species then?"

"As I remember it, we set down for a day and a half in an emergency, on a site much like this. We were too busy repairing the ship to do much exploring. But I've never forgotten the place."

No one asked why it wasn't on the chart. But I was sure I knew. And I wondered how many other planets like this, beautiful and special, remained private memories. In one way I liked the idea. But in other ways I resented knowledge being kept so secret. And I couldn't help but wonder what Caper's memory had to do with our being on the planet. Furthermore, since we had arrived, he seemed to be taking over—telling us what to do—when we were the ones who were supposed to be planning and accomplishing. He was only along to advise.

"When you were here before, did this planet have a name?" Waver, as usual, was interested in details no one else would consider.

"None that I know of," Caper said. "The sun doesn't even have a name."

"Then let's give the planet one," Waver suggested. "In my mind I've been calling it Ariel, after a good spirit in an old play. Somehow it seems to fit this place."

That was one thing Waver was good at—names. If there were a place in Discovery for a namer, Waver wouldn't have to worry about his future.

"Ariel," I said. "I like it."

"Too flighty," said Gloust. "This is a solid place."

"But Ariel seems right," Bisty said.

"Then Ariel it is," Caper agreed. "I rather like it myself."

"But if there is a minded species here," Gloust persisted, "they'll have a name for it themselves."

"Then we can change," Waver said. "But until we find them, we have to call it something."

So we called it Ariel. And that first day we went to the trees at the west and followed them south a way. A forest, Caper said it was. We picked more of the fruit we had found—it appeared in several places—and ate it in the shade of the trees, looking out over the plain. We could hardly get enough of looking, any of us.

"Should we bring the ship to the trees?" Gloust asked finally.

"Yes," said Caper. "We can find enough food along the forest edge, I think, and so far we haven't seen anything dangerous."

"What about protein?" Bisty asked. "I don't see any animals here, and the fruits we've picked don't have much."

"Ah, yes," said Waver. "Even in paradise one must have a balanced diet."

"Well, it is important," Bisty said.

"Yes, it is," said Gloust, unexpectedly. "Maybe there'll be something like fish in the streams. I made a fishhook and brought it along."

"A what?" Bisty asked.

"A fishhook," Gloust said. "You use it to catch a fish. I read about it in a book on survival."

"What else did you read?" Caper asked, obviously amused.

"How to build shelters—I told you that—and make clothes with natural materials."

"Is that possible?" Bisty asked. Life support deals largely with advance preparation—taking along what you need—not with making do in the wilds. That was Gloust's territory.

"How do you think people did it before fabrication machines?" Gloust wanted to know.

"I never thought of it," Bisty said.

"There were times long ago on Earth when people were hungry, starved to death even. They didn't worry about protein. They were happy with anything they could find to eat," Waver announced.

"And they lived in shelters made of trees or in caves," Gloust said. "One book I read told about how to make log houses. Why don't we try it while we're here?"

"You're only going to be here for two octaves," Caper reminded him. "And although I've never done much of that sort of thing, I know it would be a lot of work."

"But it would be something different. A real survival thing," Waver said. "That's what this trip is for. And it would give us some idea of what it might have been like to live on Earth a long time ago."

"Well, let's move the ship first," Caper said. "Then we'll talk about shelters."

We walked back to the ship slowly, enjoying the warm afternoon. Then just before sunset, when our movement was least likely to be noticed—if there was anyone to notice—we took the ship up and brought it down again, lightly, near the trees at the west of the plain.

We went up under gravity power. I ran the ship, and at Caper's suggestion we stayed up a bit longer than necessary, so we could all get a good idea of where we were. I couldn't see as much as the rest, but decided that my first impression was essentially correct. There was forest to the north, over rolling hills and then atop a flat mesalike plain that eventually gave way to mountains. There were forests to the west, also. And to the east the plain melded into an area of low scrubby bushes and then beyond that into forest again. To the south, the forests opened into a broader plain.

Nowhere in all that vast expanse did I see anything that made me think there were minded creatures anywhere.

"Doesn't seem to be anyone here but us," Gloust said, echoing my thoughts.

Caper smiled, an odd smile. "You can never be too sure," he said.

No one asked him what he meant. We assumed he was just advising us to be cautious.

When the ship was all buttoned up after its brief trip, we opened the upper air lock, went down the steps, and out the lower lock. It was growing dark, and the stars were coming out. Many of them had to be stars we had always known. But here in this new place they seemed different, made different configurations.

Waver expressed it exactly. "It's as if they were all made new just for us," he said. "Why don't we make our own constellations?"

Gloust laughed. "People haven't used constellations in mapping the sky for thousands of years."

"People haven't lived as we're living for thousands of years," Waver retorted. "We ought to learn the sky so we can find our way if we get lost."

"That's not a bad idea," Gloust admitted. "Though you don't need whole constellations for that—just a few beacon stars."

"Look, there's a leaf over there, like the ones on the fruit bushes." I pointed to a group of stars that, to me, fell into a leaf pattern.

"And there's a ship like ours," said Waver.

"That circle up there looks like a navithought helmet," Bisty suggested.

"You're all crazy," Gloust said.

"But we do need something to give us a sense of direction at night," Caper told him. And he proceeded to identify some of the brightest stars by their true names. But the rest of us really liked our constellations better.

We were all beginning to feel very tired by that time. It was a different tired from the one we had felt after being under the helmet. Then we were drained of energy. But this was fatigue of the muscles and bones.

"I'm ready to drop," Bisty said, which expressed it for all of us. We went into the ship and went to bed.

The days that followed were little different from that first day. Mostly, they were spent in exploring. We went north and south along the west edge of the plain. We went across the plain and explored into the bushes and trees on that side. We even contrived a makeshift compass from some of the ship's gear and went into the western forest one day, following a stream. On most of these jaunts we were all happy. Caper sang, and Gloust tramped along, lifting and pounding on things, examining everything. Waver sometimes made up stories about the things we were seeing, which he told as we moved along. It was a happy time, an enchanted time. We were all in love with Ariel.

Food was no problem. It seemed to be everywhere. There were even bushes in open places in the forest that had fruits of various sorts, most of them edible. Bisty was upset about our lack of protein until she discovered that some strange leathery disks that grew on the forest floor were edible and contained substantial amounts of protein. She insisted that we eat them, and we did, though we hated them. Finally Waver found some fruits protected by hard shells that also had protein. They tasted better than the leathery things, and Bisty let us eat them when we could find them. Secretly I thought even she was glad we had found something else.

"But why no animals?" Someone asked that question almost every day.

"A planet cannot have evolved to this state without some kind of animal life," Waver declared. We had seen some insectlike creatures. But nothing larger. Gloust had even tried his fishhook unsuccessfully.

"Maybe they only come at certain times," Gloust suggested one day when we had been on an unusually long walk and still had seen nothing.

"Or maybe they come out at night," Bisty said. "We're so tired every night. We go to bed early, and I don't think we wake up very much until morning."

"If we built a shelter, we could stay in it and maybe we'd hear something," Gloust proposed. I had thought the shelter idea was forgotten; in fact I had hoped it was. It sounded like too much work.

"Still want to build a shelter, eh?" Caper said.

"Yes, if for nothing but the experience of doing it," Gloust said.

"It might be fun," Waver agreed.

I looked at him amazed. Waver did not like heavy

101

work. Building a shelter might be good experience for Gloust. But I couldn't see what it would do for Waver.

"We'll talk about it tonight," Caper promised. "I like the idea. Now back to the ship and some food."

We gathered some edibles on the way back, moving slowly along the edge of the western forest.

"Old-time people used to dry things to make them last," Gloust said as we neared the ship.

"Really?" Bisty said. This trip was obviously teaching her a lot about life support that had nothing to do with the things she usually studied. "How do you do it?"

Gloust described the things he had read, and Bisty was determined to try it.

"But we aren't old-time people," Waver said. "And what will you do with it once you've got it dried?"

"We'll need food for the trip home, for one thing," Bisty said. "It's been worrying me. I'm not sure the things we've been eating would keep as they are in our food-storage units."

That made sense. "Why don't you three men begin work on the shelter tomorrow, if you're so determined to build one," I said. "Bisty and I will look for food and try drying it."

Bisty looked at me oddly. "I do want to do the drying," she said. "But I want to help on Gloust's shelter, too."

That wasn't like Bisty. Her life-support systems did not include log shelters, even if they could be stretched to include dried natural foods.

"You won't get lost if you two go looking for food alone?" Caper asked.

My sharp tongue had not changed. "Of course not," I said scornfully.

So that was how it was decided. And before the evening was over, we were all interested in the shelter. We talked about it in a circle on the ground in front of the ship while we watched the sun go down and the stars come out. Eventually there was also a slip of a moon, the first we had seen of one.

Gloust went over all he remembered of what he had read about shelter building. And Caper added not only some reading, but some experience. "Had to repair a ship once before we could go on, and to do that we had to pull the bunks out. So we made ourselves a place to stay outside. Not much of a place. Nothing as grand as the one Gloust plans. But it was an experience I won't forget. That planet," he finished, "had animals. Big ones."

We shuddered and tried to imagine it, but couldn't. I realized that I had never seen a live animal. There were plenty of pictures of them at the School/Home. The films that played on the walls of our exercise rooms always showed them. They actually seemed a part of my past. But they weren't.

"What shall we use to build our shelter?" Caper asked. "Which of the kinds you've described do you actually want to make, Gloust?"

"A stone foundation, with logs on top," Gloust said.

"How will you keep the stones together?"

"Mud, I think," Gloust said. "The right kind will dry hard and hold stones in place."

He and Waver began then to work out what should be done. They would use stones, held together by mud, for a foundation. The walls would be tree logs, lashed together with supple branches or fitted together with notches. Gloust had evidently read very widely.

103

When we went into the ship finally, later than usual, Gloust and Waver stood over the chart desk, making a drawing of their shelter, while I updated the log and Bisty made plans for gathering and drying food.

Just as I was starting toward my bunk, Caper turned to me and said, "I wish you'd look at the control-guidance system someday, especially the gravity engines. Didn't they seem a little sluggish the day we moved the ship here? They may have been tired. But it's worth a glance."

I didn't remember sensing that when I moved the ship, but Caper did have more experience with the feel of gravity movement than I did. He could be right. It wouldn't hurt to check. I didn't think more of it until, as I opened the door to my bunk, Waver came up and put his hand on my shoulder.

"Check it tomorrow," he said in a low voice. Then glancing back at Caper, he added, "And if you wake up early, go outside. I'll try to be there, too."

A swift beam of fear shot through me. I had almost forgotten my worry about Caper. Life on Ariel had been so absorbing that it had driven everything else out of my mind. But obviously Waver still had some questions.

I settled into my bunk, wondering if I should begin worrying again. But then I decided I didn't know what to worry about, except the ship's guidance system. And, remembering the tools I had hidden aboard, I felt confident I could fix anything that was wrong. Besides, I was too sleepy to stay awake.

10

I woke up almost as sharply as if someone had knocked on my door and said, "Get up." And it was no surprise to find Waver at the ship's lower door. He nodded, smiled, and we quietly let ourselves out. The sun was just up, and the land around was as beautiful as I had ever seen it.

As I stepped away from the ship, I thought I caught a bit of movement in the distance, at the edge of the forest where it curved into the plain to the north. But it was so slight, and the distance so great, I knew I could well be mistaken.

Still, I grabbed Waver's arm and pointed. "Did you see something move? Up there, by the trees?"

"Did you really think there was only plant life here?" he asked.

"No, not really. But we haven't seen anything else."

"We've been too noisy." He sounded very sure.

"Everything is frightened away before we get to it. You know how Caper sings and Gloust thunders along. And I've added to it with my stories. On purpose, I might add."

I didn't understand what he meant. Waver often tested his ideas in ways only he could grasp. The noise I knew about. But the thought that creatures might be frightened away hadn't occurred to me. And I wasn't sure what he had been trying to accomplish with his stories.

"Is any of the life intelligent?"

"Maybe," Waver said.

"But would they be afraid, too?"

"If they've never seen a ship like ours before. But it's not the animals, or even intelligent life, that I'm afraid of. It's the life we have with us. Did it ever occur to you, Rom, that we may never leave here?"

The idea split me in two like a laser beam. Part of me loved it, and part of me hated it. But certainly I hadn't thought of it before. "What makes you say that!"

"Who's been here before?"

"Caper."

"Who suggested that there might be something wrong with the ship?"

"Caper."

"Who's building a shelter?"

"Gloust and Caper, but you agreed with them."

"Yes, partly because I did think it would be a good experience, and partly because I wanted to see what might happen. Gloust is in love with this place, with life here, you know."

I did know. And I was in love with it myself. It

seemed as if I had come home. "What are you trying to tell me?"

"I wish I could be more specific. We've both suspected Caper of wanting something from this trip, and we both know he loves this place and has been here before. Now there's this thing with the ship. It all fits together, somehow. And I get the feeling that he's looking for something. But I don't know what."

Now that Waver had said it, I could see it, too. First Caper had suggested our looking over the landscape while we moved the ship. Then every day we had explored in a different direction. Which might seem natural. But somehow it had been done in too systematic a way. Even the noise might be a part of it. It wasn't like Caper to sing.

"Did he plan to come here all along?" I asked. "How could he? We decided to come here before he got back from his trip!" But then I remembered the hint he had given; 22 could have been his idea.

"The terms of the trip all but sent us here," Waver said. "Did you ever wonder why the school would think up something like this? We weren't ready for this kind of jaunt. And I can't really believe that mess with Keery Soter would create this much revenge. Nothing in writing ever said we had to find uninhabited planets. Only Caper said that."

It was true. "Then any planet would have done, even one with people, just so long as it had some wild areas?"

"It's possible."

I sat down on the ground. In a way I didn't blame Caper. This was a great place, and I could understand why he might want to come back. But to stay! We weren't prepared for that, no matter how much Gloust had read about wilderness survival and how much Caper knew about edible plants. Besides, even Caper had said that five people could not colonize a planet. Yet, Waver just might be right.

I felt suddenly sick, not so much at the idea that Caper might want us to stay, as at the idea that we might have been used. Caper might have taken advantage of us. He might even have deliberately made us sick with those plants just for an excuse to bring us here. We had been so determined to do what the committee asked, and to do it ourselves, that making us sick may have seemed the only way to get us to take his advice. But had he really been so desperate to get here? And was he as desperate to stay?

"I could be wrong," Waver said. "Don't say anything, and we'll see what happens. We don't really know what Caper has in mind, so there's no use borrowing trouble. Just be cautious, and be sure to check that guidance system."

"I'll check it today," I told him. "But surely Caper wouldn't really damage the ship, would he?"

"Just enough to make it impossible to leave, I suppose," Waver said.

"There are some things that are easy to break, but not easy to fix."

"Exactly. Now let's go over to the stream and look for mud. I think I saw some there that might dry into a fairly solid cement."

By the time the others were up, we had not only found Waver's mud, but had tossed together a pile of stones that might make a beginning for the foundation of the shelter. We were wet and dirty, but exhilarated. And I was amused at Waver. He had been having such fun trying a new idea. It's only when he knows that something will work that he gets tired of it. Until then, he's willing to do anything. Though generally he looks for less physical activities.

After all that exercise, we were both more than ready for breakfast. We ate as if we had never seen food before.

"If the kind of work you three are going to do today is going to make you that hungry," Bisty said, "there won't be any point in drying what food we find. We'll need it all just for today."

Caper laughed. "If it comes to that, we'll stop building the shelter to help feed ourselves."

A little later, Bisty and I set out along the edge of the forest, moving south. It was another lovely day, and the freedom of being able to choose what we would do, to move in the sweet-smelling air, was glorious. The idea of staying on Ariel had appeal. But at the same time, I knew if we did, we would face unimaginable hardships and dangers.

Bisty seemed more lost in thought that morning than she usually was. I wondered if she would really have preferred to help with the shelter. And then I realized that just as I had begun to enjoy Waver's company more than usual, she had been spending more time with Gloust. We were pairing off! The thought gave me a jolt. People didn't do that until they were seventeen or eighteen.

As we walked in silence, each with our own

thoughts, I thought I saw movement around us several times. Eventually we found a few clumps of fruit. Some of it was not quite ripe, but there was plenty ready for picking. We chose good, firm fruits in the hope that they would keep best. When our carriers were nearly full, we went into the forest a little way to look for some of the protein plants. It was in the forest that I said, quite unexpectedly even to myself, "Would you like to stay here forever?"

Bisty looked at me almost in horror. "Oh, no! I like it well enough for now. But not forever, even if that is what Gloust and the rest of you would like." She stopped, then started again. "I like to have a lot of people around. And you know it's life-support systems I care about—developing them, not running around the galaxy using them. Once in a while I'd like to go on a trip to try something out. And you can get some good ideas from having to exist on a place like this for a while. But I don't want to be in space all the time."

I nodded my head, then told her about Waver's suspicions.

"But, Rom, we'd all go crazy. We'd have to spend all of our time on food and clothes and shelter. There'd be no book cards, no laboratories—nothing really interesting."

"There are other things to make up for what isn't here," I said. "Freedom, quiet, the beautiful out-of-doors. Being able to walk like this."

She looked at me with alarm, and I quickly added, "But I don't want to stay. Five people can't settle a planet and survive. And Caper must know that. Besides, it would be bad for the School/Home. We do owe

110

them something, and it's not right to steal their expensive ship, which is what we would be doing."

"Can Caper keep us from going back, if that's what he wants to do?" Bisty asked.

"He could make it hard for us," I admitted. "Especially if he should convince Gloust to stay with him. We really need four under the helmet. And I don't know if there is anything wrong with the ship or not."

"Listen, our carrying cases are almost full. There's more fruit ripe now than when we first came. Let's go back. I'll try the drying, and you can check the ship. And Rom, should I talk to Gloust, see how he feels about staying here?"

I thought about that for a moment. Bisty was certainly the one to ask him, if he should be asked. But I didn't know how close he had become to Caper. If Caper should hear of our suspicions, and there was basis for them, our problems might increase. I shook my head. "Not yet," I said.

Back at the ship, Bisty worked just outside, spreading her fruits and roots and the protein plants in the sun, after cutting them into small pieces. Then, for our night meal, she began some cooking. We had been eating everything raw; but Bisty, after consulting Gloust and his reading, had decided to try cooking some things together.

I glanced at her occasionally through the viewport while I examined the guidance system. It was sluggish enough to create problems under the helmet as well as under gravity drive. Yet I was sure it had not been that way the day I moved the ship. I began to search for the cause; and when I found it, I was glad I had brought some extra tools. Some small connections had been destroyed, and it took all the skill and equipment I had to fix them. It was impossible to tell if it had happened naturally or if someone had done it. I had never heard of those particular connections failing, but then there were a lot of things I had never heard of. If Caper had done it, though, I wondered why he had mentioned it. Had he wanted me to discover the problem, be unable to fix it, and then to suggest that we all stay? I decided not to mention what I had done. I would just pretend I had forgotten.

When Bisty and I were both finished with our jobs, we went to see how the shelter was coming. The three had accomplished a lot. They were working near the stream, about 250 meters from the ship, but hidden from it by a small hill. Using the ground explorer, they had leveled a flat space and removed the grasses from it. Then they had dug a shallow trench around the outside, and into this they had placed a row of the largest rocks they could find. The top of the stones had been leveled off with mud, and now they were putting a layer of smaller stones into that mud.

"This will take a day or two to dry," Caper said. "And while that's going on, we'll be cutting our trees and getting them ready."

"It looks great," Bisty said. "But isn't it a little small for the five of us?"

"Well, we're not going to be here forever," Waver said. "The important thing is to do it—to see if it works. And we can take turns using it, if we want to."

"If we like the first, we can always build a second, even a third," Gloust said.

"You can," Waver said, grinning. "One will be enough for me."

"Besides, we don't have all that much time," I pointed out. "I checked the log today. We're almost at the end of the second octave."

Neither Caper nor Gloust answered, but they exchanged a furtive look that the rest of us all saw. Obviously there was some secret between Gloust and Caper. I felt a sudden twinge of real alarm.

"By the way," Waver said, to change the subject, "when Rom and I were out here this morning, we thought we saw something move in the distance, like an animal."

"I thought I saw something once or twice when Bisty and I went south this morning, too," I announced. "There was some kind of movement that wasn't the wind." Might as well see what reaction that would bring.

"I didn't see anything," Bisty said. "Why didn't you say something?"

"It may have been because we were quiet that I saw it," I explained.

"I'm sure there are animals," Caper said. "There have to be. And it may be that we have frightened them away with our noise. Maybe when our shelter is ready, some of us can hide inside and we'll get a better picture of what's here."

And that was that on the subject of animals, mostly because we were all tired and hungry. Bisty's cooking experiment turned out very well. Gloust, especially, had good things to say, and Bisty glowed with pleasure. But after the evening meal, there was no star gazing. The

113

constellations we had picked out were not doing us much good. We were too tired at night to use them.

Suddenly I began wondering about that, too. Was there some reason we were having all this activity that left us so exhausted? It really wasn't necessary. And a little time to watch the stars at night might have been fun. It was Caper who had kept us going so much, though all of us had wanted to explore. Did he want us sleeping heavily at night, going to bed early, or was I just getting too suspicious? After all, there were easier ways to put us to sleep than wearing us all out.

I don't know how long I had been asleep that night when I was startled awake by a soft noise from outside. I suppose because I had been wondering about animals, my subconscious had been more aware than usual of the noises around. Whatever the reason, upon awaking, I stole out of my bunk and moved to a small viewport. Starlight and the light of the moon, now almost full, brightened the landscape.

Watching carefully, I was gradually aware of movement in our area. Small winged creatures flitted out now and then from the forest. But more than that! Something stood near the edge of the forest, something just a little bit taller than I, on two legs, with arms not unlike mine.

A winged creature dove down and came up with something in its mouth. As my eye followed the action, the two-legged creature disappeared.

It was true then that the creatures of this world came out at night! But why? Surely the day was more pleasant. And why were so few of the fruits picked by the creatures who lived here? Was there some danger on the plain and near it that they knew and the five of us did not? And what was the two-legged creature? Was it minded? Was it dangerous?

I went back to bed, but did not sleep immediately. For the first time on the entire trip, worry kept me awake.

The others would not believe me in the morning, not even Waver.

"You've got animals on the brain," Gloust said. "Winged ones I can accept. But not two-legged ones."

"You were dreaming, Rom," Waver said. "It was all that talk about movement yesterday."

"Well, don't believe me then," I said. "But look yourself some night."

In spite of the general lack of belief, Bisty was not eager to go too far in search of food. We picked near the ship and the new house. Then when the food being dried had been laid out again, and some more cooked for meals that day, we helped the others bring in the trees their laser protectors had cut. Using some impromptu wheels, portions of logs cut from a tree, and an axle made of a tree limb shoved through laser-made holes at the center of each wheel, we pulled the logs to the house site and trimmed away branches that had not been trimmed before. Gloust said these would make a roof.

Gloust had really studied those books on shelter making. He knew just what to do, and he seemed happier than we had ever seen him. Not full of tricks to ward off boredom, or silent, just doing and saying what was needed. He belongs in a place like this, I found myself

115

thinking. But wasn't that just what his training at the School/Home was preparing him for—exploration of places like this?

The next two days tended to fall into much the same pattern. Bisty and I would hunt food each morning and go on with the drying of what we did not need. Then the rest of the day we would help with the shelter. By the end of the second day, the walls were up and a network of branches had been crosshatched over the top to make a foundation for the still smaller branches and leaves that would form the roof. On the third day, we wove mats of small, supple branches to lay on the network we had installed. The mats we put up the morning of the next day. And on top of the mats, we laid large leathery leaves we had found. Bisty and I did the work of actually putting the leaves on the roof because we were lighter, and the boys and Caper filled the places between the logs below with mud. Then it was finished. It had taken six days altogether to make the shelter. And I figured we were into the last day of the pause before the third octave of our stay away from the School/Home.

"Shall we spend the night here?" asked Gloust.

"I think not," said Caper. "We still don't have a door, and we might need one. Protection from those monsters Rom saw."

Everyone laughed but me. I had not seen anything again. But maybe only because I had been too tired to stay awake or to wake up. Building a shelter was hard work. But I knew what I had seen. And I was still a little frightened by it.

"Let's not wait," Gloust pleaded. "There's nothing to hurt us here."

"Better to be safe," said Caper. "We'll make a door tomorrow, and then we'll see about spending the night."

That night, as I dictated to the log, I realized that we had only one octave and a pause, at most, before we had to be back at the School/Home. Eleven or twelve days. It seemed a long time. And yet it also seemed far too short, especially if I might never see a place like this again.

We had been too busy to talk about Caper and leaving, Waver and Bisty and I. Too busy to think. But whether that was Caper's planning or our own fault, I didn't know. And there was really nothing we could do about the situation until Caper, or perhaps Gloust, said or did something to indicate that our suspicions had some foundation. I knew, of course, that whatever happened, we had to try to go back to the School/Home, though I did wish it seemed more attractive to me. We could not stay on Ariel. Five people could not settle a planet, no matter what was or was not there in the way of animal life. Yet with every day, I had come to love Ariel more. It was a glorious place.

11

The next day, once we had the door on, we celebrated the completion of the shelter with a picnic. As we sat looking at our accomplishment, we even gave it a name, Treerock. It wasn't very poetic, but at least it told what the place was made of.

In the afternoon we strolled off into the forest, along the stream. Caper got ahead of us, and Waver and I wandered off to look at a tree that seemed hollow, thinking it might be the lair of some animal.

"Not a two-legged one, though," Waver teased.

I grinned at him. "You'll see. Someday you'll regret your lack of faith." Actually, I was beginning to wonder about what I had really seen, myself.

"I don't know about lack of faith," he said. "Just lack of corroborating evidence."

He took my hand, and we ran back to the stream.

Gloust and Bisty were deep in conversation, so the two of us went on together. And I decided to broach the other subject that had bothered me—why we were pairing off at our ages. It was a little awkward to begin. I didn't quite know how to start. But I felt sure Waver had sensed it, too. So I simply tried to explain, as matter-of-factly as I could, what I had observed and how I felt.

We stopped and sat down finally, leaning against a tree. Waver didn't say anything, and I was embarrassed, afraid that maybe I had overstated the situation.

But then Waver took my hand again; he turned it back and forth between his hands.

"Yes, I know," he said finally. "I've felt it, too. I've tried not to. That's part of why I've been working so hard. It didn't seem natural. We're too young. But now I've decided that maybe we're not. Maybe people are supposed to feel like this at our age. Maybe the School/Home does something to keep us from . . . you know. All of a sudden at eighteen or so, everyone pairs off. But maybe it . . . well, maybe they give us something that we're not getting on this trip."

We sat a while longer, enjoying being near each other. Waver put his arm around my shoulder, and I put my head on his. It was very comfortable. In fact I didn't know when I had been so full of contentment, except that something kept making me want to move even closer. It was clear why the School/Home prevented this, if they did. We all lived too close together, already.

"The dessert energy-bars!" I said suddenly, sitting straight up. "They wanted us to take a three-octave supply, and Bisty sent most of them back."

Waver sat up, too, looking at me, and then we both howled with laughter. It was all so clear. Waver pulled me back finally, kissed me, and then, not daring to explore our feelings further, we stood up and ran to find the others.

"Shall we tell them?" I asked.

"No," Waver said. "Not unless it looks as if things are getting out of hand between Gloust and Bisty."

"Not between us," I said, teasing again.

"Our superior sense will see us through until we get back to the dessert energy-bars," he said.

"That sounds a little grim," I told him. We grinned at each other and ran along the stream, back to the shelter.

The others arrived soon after—as far as we could tell, none the worse for the venture. When I talked to Bisty later, I decided that Gloust had spent most of the time they were together pointing out the glories of Ariel.

"I wish I could like this planet as much as he does," Bisty said, sighing. "But I don't think I ever will. It's nice, but it's dull."

Caper and Gloust spent that night in the shelter. The next morning they were full of enthusiasm for log-house living.

"Why don't we build another, so all of us can stay out here?" Gloust said. "You can't imagine how nice it is."

"We could take turns in the one we have," I pointed out.

"Not me," said Bisty. "A leaf mattress on the ground is not my idea of comfort."

"Spoiled by years of soft living," Gloust said, teasing her.

"Well, we all are," Waver muttered.

"I'm with Bisty," I said. "I can see all I want to see of this planet in the daytime. And there's room enough for Waver here if he wants to spend the night."

In the end it was three against one. There would be no new shelter built.

Caper said nothing, but he did not seem displeased with our decision. Yet, if he wanted to stay here, surely another shelter would be useful. What game was he playing? Or were the games all in our minds? I felt like suggesting that we begin getting ready to go home, but didn't dare. I wanted to know what would happen, and yet I didn't.

That day Caper suggested that we all walk south along the forest. We went further than Bisty and I had gone, and we all picked whatever we found that was edible. For once, we were quiet, and at last we saw some animals, all very small, but animals nevertheless. At the first one, we just stopped and stared. No matter how well you know that other living creatures live, the first time you actually see one close, it's a shock. And perhaps it was as much of a shock to that small furry being to have five great two-legged creatures staring down at it. At any rate it ran away in a hurry.

Ariel was an endlessly fascinating place, I decided then, as I often had before. And as before, I wondered about Earth. Was it like this? Did all of us like this place because something in us remembered; did it call us back to the kind of place our ancestors had known? Had my parents ever felt this way on planets they explored?

It was a long walk, and we came back dusty and dry and tired. But we made a fire near the house and cooked dinner, and afterwards we sat around the fire as it grew dark. I looked up at the stars, and they seemed far away, too remote ever to reach.

"Where's Earth, Earth's sun that is?" Waver asked suddenly, and I realized that his thoughts must have been following mine.

"Can't see it from here with the unaided eye," Caper said. "Over that way." He pointed to the east.

"I'd like to see Earth sometime," Waver said.

"Why?" asked Caper. "What you've got here is better."

The words were innocent enough, but the strength with which they were spoken made me afraid again.

"Have you been to Earth?" Bisty asked.

"You know I haven't! But I've seen pictures," he said. "And I've talked to people who have been. A strange place, our mother planet. Too wrapped up in itself; selfish, in a way. But then that's not the greatest sin in the galaxy, I guess." He yawned and stretched. "That walk did me in. Do you feel as tired as I do?"

"It's the sun," Bisty said. "I've been reading one of the books we have along about health. You have to be careful when you're not used to a sun. It not only burns, but it makes you tired. It's good for you, though, I think."

"It certainly puts me to sleep, if that's what's doing it," Caper murmured. But there was that artificial quality in his voice that made me question the truth of what he said. Besides, Caper had been around enough not to have to wonder. He ought to know. I looked at Waver, and he looked at me.

"I'm ready for the old bed myself," Waver declared.

"And may I say that in spite of your offer of space here and a desire to test the night air of Ariel, I look forward to retiring on my air mattress in the ship. Enjoy your leaves, fellows."

We all laughed, and Bisty and I got up to join him.

"See you in the morning," Caper said, still laughing.

"Softies," Gloust shouted after us. But there was a laugh in his voice, too.

"Listen, we've just got to talk," Waver said. "I don't know what's happening, and I'm scared."

"Why scared?" Bisty asked. "Rom says that maybe Gloust and Caper want to stay here. But they can't, can they?"

"There's no way we can make them get on the ship," Waver pointed out.

"And this ship is hard for us to run with four," I pointed out. "I'm not sure we could make it back with three. Besides, if we go back without them, we'll have to tell where they are, and someone might come to get them. They won't want that."

"They'd be pretty hard to find if they wanted to get lost," Waver said.

"I can't stay here; I'd go out of my mind!" Bisty said. "I think we should ask Caper and Gloust what's going on. Surely Gloust, at least, wouldn't make us stay if we didn't want to."

"Not a good idea," I told her. "One of two things could happen. Either we might not get the truth, or we might get more truth than we wanted, and then we'd find our chances of getting home even slighter."

"Rom's right," Waver agreed. "All we can do is watch and plan."

"Watch what?" I asked. "Nothing happens. Except that Caper isn't always telling the truth."

"Something will happen soon," Waver said.

"Not tonight, I hope," Bisty told him. "I'm too tired."

We were all three in our bunks in a hurry. The long walk really had tired us. Again I wondered if Caper had worn us out on purpose. Or did he take us on these walks just to look for whatever he was looking for? I was too sleepy to think beyond that.

In the middle of the night, however, I woke up with the same kind of bumping sound over my head that had awakened me before. Another night bird, I thought sleepily. And half-awake, I wondered if night birds always meant two-legged creatures at the edge of the forest. It was logical, I supposed. The birds, or whatever they were, were disturbed and came flying out. I didn't want to get up, but I did.

There was still a moon, and the landscape was quite bright. I looked toward the hill that hid the shelter, and thought I saw something move at the edge of the forest in that direction.

Where were the field glasses? I didn't dare turn on any lights aboard. What cupboard? What shelf? I fumbled hastily, and then dropped something. That brought Waver out.

"Something over by the forest," I whispered, as if my voice might disturb whoever it was. "Looking for binoculars."

He understood at once.

"Not there. Here." He went to the chart cupboard and pulled out not one but two pairs.

"We all put in some extra gear," he said.

We hurried back to the port and realized that there was no question about it. Even before we had our glasses focused, we knew that there was someone there! And that someone was a thinking being very much like the two of us; and it was not Caper or Gloust.

Once our glasses were focused, we decided it could only be someone whose heritage was Earth. The look was unmistakable, even though the clothes were strange. And then, while we were still amazed by that, we saw Caper come around the hill! We waited for Gloust, but he didn't appear. The two people—Caper and whoever else it was—talked for some time. The stranger gestured once up the plain. Was that where he had come from? Or was the conversation about something else? Waver and I looked on without a whisper. I didn't know what he felt, but a senseless terror had seized me. What complications did this new person add to our problems?

Finally Caper walked back behind the hill, and the person disappeared into the forest.

"Well, that answers two things," Waver said slowly. "You were right. And now we know what to fear: other people."

There was nothing to add, and still no way to calculate what the future might hold. Sleep was actually what we needed most. We should be rested to face whatever the morning might bring. So we went to our bunks, I, at least, trembling and cold.

Once there, I couldn't sleep. My mind was too full of questions. If there was one person, there had to be more—quite a few more. I remembered Caper's saying that five people could not colonize a planet. Obviously

Earth ships had come here in the past and left people behind—or maybe the ships had just stayed and were hidden. But in either case, the people were not here legally. Earth did not colonize habitable planets. And this planet was not even on the charts. These had to be people who had just gone off and disappeared. Discoverers who had vanished! Was that what had happened to so many? Were they all here? Or were there a lot of secret colonies? And had Caper known?

I finally went to sleep, dreaming of people who lived inside the trunks of trees, and people who made homes in caves—people who had no children because they had left them behind.

The next morning we talked briefly about what we had seen. Day chased away the worst of my terror, and I could talk rationally with the others. But I did tell them of my idea about lost Discoverers.

Waver had thought of that, too. "We'd better not leave the ship unguarded," he said. "If they are Discoverers, they'll know too much about it. Not that they'll want to steal it, I suppose. But they won't want us to leave and tell people back at the School/Home that they're here. We don't want them tampering with the controls. The next time Rom might not be able to fix the damage."

"How many days before we should go?" Bisty asked.

"If only three of us are going," I said, "then we shouldn't stay more than four days, five at the most. It'll take us a long time to get home, if we make it at all."

"And if four go?" she asked.

"Six days here, and no problems," I assured her.

"Let me look at the oxygen," she said, moving to the gauge.

126

Trust Bisty to remember what was really important.

"Half full," she reported. "I'll turn on the machine. Caper has no idea of how much dried food we have, so I'll just put most of it in the food-storage boxes. But what about water?"

The water tanks, too, were only half full.

"Why don't we suggest that you and I, Rom, go over to the east side of the plain to pick today," Bisty suggested. "I can say I want to try drying the berries that are there. We can bring water from that side then, and it won't be so obvious."

"It's a lot farther to carry it," Waver said. "I'll try to get some from this side, too, if I can. I'll say we need to do some cleaning up inside the ship. It's not a lie," he added, looking around.

That was about all we could plan because we had no idea of what would happen when we met Caper and Gloust.

As we left the ship, I looked to the north and noticed that the horizon was dusty, hazy. There had been no rain since we came, and the days had all been sharp and clear. But there must be rain sometime. Yet the haze did not seem to suggest rain, even to someone like me who had never seen it.

"Remember the plan," Waver said. "We must get water."

All three of us approached the shelter with a sense of dread that morning. We had no idea of what was coming. But what happened was the most unexpected of all: nothing. Caper and Gloust behaved exactly the way they always did. Further, Caper was completely open to the suggestion that Bisty and I gather fruit on the other side of the plain. And Waver was able to bring water to the ship with no awkward questions asked. Caper and Gloust, themselves, went into the forest looking for protein.

In the afternoon, with our chores done, the five of us actually had fun. We played games, made up riddles, and in general relaxed, or seemed to. For the three of us, relaxing was partly pretending.

Caper seemed more at ease, more himself, than he had been in some time. Maybe, I thought, that was because he had at last achieved some goal he had in mind and now knew just what he wanted to do. Though whether meeting with someone who lived on the planet had been that goal, I had no way of knowing.

When night came, we sat and talked for a long time because we were not so tired as we had been—the day had not been as difficult as some. We looked at the sky, and now everyone noticed the haze I had seen in the morning. It had grown worse. We couldn't see the stars as clearly as we had before.

"Maybe it will be clearer later tonight," Caper said. "Why don't you all stay out here? It's warm, and we don't all need to be in the shelter. Rom and Bisty can stay inside if they like. And Gloust and Waver and I can just sleep on the ground outside."

"Not me," I said. "If there's one thing I've discovered on this trip, it's that I only like to rough it in comfort." That wasn't entirely true. But this was not the night to stay at the shelter.

"That goes for me, too," Bisty said. And I knew she meant it.

"And I've got some reading I have to do tonight," Waver said. "I'm way behind on the book cards I brought."

Caper and Gloust both laughed.

"Some pioneers!" Gloust taunted.

"Try it out here just once," Caper urged. "You'll like it."

They tried hard to persuade us, and at one point I thought that if they could have held us there by force, they would have. Caper was especially determined. But we remained unconvinced, and in the end we went off to the ship, and they stayed behind.

12

It was the middle of the night, and there was a familiar bump. Or was it familiar? It sounded more like something bumping the ship near the ground than up near the cabin. Maybe not a bird this time. A second bump followed the first, and I decided to get up.

I was not the first at a viewport this time. Waver and Bisty were there ahead of me. The moon was not so bright as it had been the night before, but there was light enough to see that the whole plain to the north was a lazily moving haze of something: animals, we realized almost at once. Some of them had struck the ship, not on purpose, just in passing.

It had never occurred to me that so many animals could exist on one planet. And I had never considered size. These animals were large—most of them a meter or more high—and they were sturdy creatures, heavy and solid. One alone could not do much damage to the ship, perhaps, but pressure from the whole group could certainly do enough damage to make the ship incapable of controlled flight. And that would certainly mean we could not take it home.

All of these things went through my mind before it occurred to me that we were, at that moment, in real physical danger. The ship could be overturned.

"We've got to do something," I screamed.

Waver was already starting to move.

"The lasers," he said. "Where are they?"

Two of our lasers were in the shelter, but we still had two on the ship.

"In the gear cupboard," Bisty said, running to open it.

There were two emergency hatches, fortunately, both quite a distance above the ground. One was on the side to the north. Waver threw it open while Bisty and I grabbed the lasers, rushed to the opening, and turned them on.

The start of the main body of the herd was about fifty meters from us. The sides of the ship were being bumped almost continually by individual animals in the more widely spaced vanguard, but none of them had hit us head-on. The herd seemed to be moving easily, slowly, spread across the entire plain. And all of the beasts seemed to be eating whatever lay in front of them as they went.

The curved sides of the ship tended to divert the flow around us; but we were afraid that when the animals became more densely packed, they might press directly against the ship and tip it over. So we shone the laser beams down in such a way that any animal that came directly toward us would be hit. This not only directed the animals away, but built up a barrier of those we were forced to kill, which diverted those behind even more. The herd moved in a leisurely way, continuing to browse on the grasses of the plain and also on the bushes and brush at the edges of the forests. None of the creatures seemed to enter the forest proper.

The assault went on and on.

"Will it never end?" Bisty asked, finally.

"Enjoy it," Waver said. "It's a fascinating phenomenon."

Right then I could have done with less fascination. It was impossible to tell how long the siege would last, because the atmosphere had become so dusty. The open hatch let the dust in, and we coughed and sputtered with it. Obviously the ground would be bare when the herd had passed.

"It's a good thing we got water," Bisty said. "Our sources may be contaminated by morning."

"How much food do we have?" I asked.

"We could use more," Bisty said. "There's enough for three or four days. Maybe five."

I nodded. Enough to get home. And for the first time I wondered about Caper and Gloust. What was happening to them? They were closer to the forest than we. Probably they were sheltering in the trees, where the animals did not seem to go. It was then that I remembered Caper's insistence that we spend the night out there. Had he known this would happen? Had Gloust? The person who had come out of the forest the night before, had he known? He had gestured to the north. If we had not been on the ship, it would almost certainly have been put out of commission. And then we would almost certainly have had to stay on Ariel.

It was nearly morning before the herd of beasts was past. The air hung heavy with the odor of their bodies and the dust they had stirred up. The beauty of the place had been destroyed. Yet I could not help but believe that this had happened before and would again. The beauty I had loved when I first stepped off the ship would return.

I remembered back to that early trip, that first journey by myself to find food. I had felt then that this was paradise. That life might never again bring me to such a perfect place. What had changed? Why did I want to go? I knew all the arguments I had made. But they were all in my mind and not in the core of my wanting. Bisty did not want to stay because she wanted to invent complicated life-support equipment. Waver did not want to stay because he needed all the knowledge of the past around him—he wanted to learn it all, whether it would ever be of any use to him or not.

But what did I want? I liked operating and repairing ships, figuring out what navigation scanners had to tell me. But did I want to do that over and over again forever? I could design and build ships, perhaps. But would even that be enough? I had been born on an uninhabited planet; Ariel was more my heritage than anything the School/Home could offer. I could survive here, if there were other people. And I could enjoy it, love it even. It would offer challenges that Discovery could not—basic, primary challenges that could make every day different. Besides, there was the sun and the wind and the feeling of being free that Ariel gave me. So did I really want to go? Yes, but maybe only because Waver and Bisty wanted to go and because it still did not seem right to stay and keep that glorious Q101 there unused.

Deep inside I was confused. I could understand Caper and Gloust too well. As we all went to bed for a few hours, I was still mixed up. I would have to make a choice soon, and I had come to realize that I wasn't ready for it. Whether I stayed or went, I stood to lose as well as gain.

Waver, knocking at my door, brought me out of dreams of vast plains and endless forests.

"Get up, Rom! No lazing about. Progress demands attention."

I roared with laughter. The last was a typical School/ Home slogan.

"Right with you," I shouted. I dressed quickly and joined Waver and Bisty for a hasty breakfast. We discussed Caper and Gloust, and decided they were in the forest, safe and waiting for us.

Before we left the ship, we looked out to make sure the animals were gone. Only one or two old stragglers were left. There seemed to be no danger.

"The dead animals!" Bisty cried. "The ones we killed. Most of them are gone!"

If we still needed it, that disappearance was proof that there were actually many people around. It had to have taken at least ten or twelve strong people, plus some kind of conveyance, to remove all of those dead animals in the few hours we had slept. Gloust and Caper could not possibly have done it alone. Nor, we realized, could it have been done without their knowledge, unless they had fled further into the forest than we thought likely. The time for decision had come.

There was nothing to do, now, but to go out and face our problem. We did not want to leave without Caper and Gloust unless we had to. In fact, we were not at all certain we could make it back to the School/Home with just the three of us. And at the back of my mind there was also the question of what I really wanted and why. Things were too complicated. I moved without thinking.

We locked the ship carefully, and I took the key. The ground, as we set off in the direction of the shelter, was rough and foul smelling. The air was heavy and hazy in all directions. The walk was not a pleasant one.

Moving over the hill, we saw that the shelter had not survived. The pressure of the beasts surging against it had pushed it off base. But it was not destroyed, simply battered, and the roof partially collapsed. It was clear that Caper and Gloust could have survived in the house. But neither of them was around.

"What now?" Waver asked.

"Progress demands attention," I said. "Look at the footprints."

Bisty grinned. "Shall we go?"

"Only to the edge of the trees," Waver said. "We need to keep an eye on the ship."

Bisty and I nodded. The ship was our most important consideration right then, if we intended to go home.

When we did not find Caper and Gloust nearby in the forest, Bisty insisted on gathering more food, if the animals had left any. She and I went into the forest with

135

gathering cases and did fill them. The animals had not penetrated the trees. Eventually we returned to Waver and then to the ship with the food. We just stored it inside and left, locking the ship up behind us. Again I took the key.

We two had just walked back to the edge of the forest when Gloust and Caper arrived. I saw them first because I was looking into the forest. Bisty and Waver were watching the ship.

"Where have you been?" I shouted. "We've been worried about you."

"Looking for a new place to stay," Gloust shouted back. "And we've found it. A huge cave in a hill, way back in there. With all kinds of things we can eat growing around it."

"A cave!" Bisty walked over to confront Gloust. "That's worst than a log house and a leaf mattress."

"You'll like it, Bisty," said Gloust, almost pleadingly. "If you let yourself, you'll feel free here. And the cave is big. We can build another shelter, of course. But not right now. And not here."

"Where then?" said Waver. "And why? We have the ship."

Gloust looked confused for a moment. As if he had said something he shouldn't have said. He gave a short, embarrassed laugh before he went on.

"Well, you know, there's really no point in leaving here. If we become Discoverers, we'll all end up in a place like this anyway. Caper says that's what's really happened to most of the Discoverers who've disappeared. They found a place like this and just stayed. So why not stay now?"

"Because the primitive life isn't what I want," Waver insisted. "No matter what I have to do for Discovery, I want to be where there are book cards and people with ideas. This is great for a vacation, but not forever."

"You know I don't want to explore planets," Bisty said plaintively. "I want to invent things, organize things, help other people explore. But I like comfort and a settled place, myself. I'd go crazy here."

"What about you, Rom?" Caper looked very serious.

"I—I don't know," I said. "I thought until last night that I had to go home. Then I realized that if we hadn't found a way to keep those animals off—"

"It would have been better if you hadn't been so clever," Caper commented wryly.

"Well, if we hadn't been able to go home, I wouldn't have minded. I was born in a place like this, and I like it. But I feel bad about Waver and Bisty. And I don't know what those other people will be like, how it will be to live here with them."

Caper looked shocked. Did he think, especially with all the dead animals gone, that we didn't know there were others here?

"We saw you with someone from here, at the edge of the woods, the other night," I said firmly. "Now, to get back to me. I loved it here from the first. It's free, as Gloust said. But I didn't want to think about staying when I thought we'd be alone. Five can't colonize a planet. But when there are others . . ." I had more to say, but Waver and Bisty were looking at me with such hostility I didn't go on.

"If that's how you feel, Rom," said Waver, quietly, "why didn't you say so earlier?"

137

"Because I have never been quite sure. It's something I've been trying to work out for myself."

"Thanks a lot," he murmured.

I would have made some sort of reply. I hated to have him angry. But suddenly my mind froze. Waver and Bisty had their backs to the forest, and behind them, out of nowhere, came three men with great sacks. I was barely aware of this before the sacks were thrown over the two of them.

There were three men, dressed in what looked like handwoven cloth made of some sort of natural fibers. The bags were of the same sort of material. No one would smother in them, but they would be rough and uncomfortable.

Waver and Bisty must have been more startled than I, because they were trapped before they could start to struggle. By the time they knew what was happening, it was too late.

"We'll leave you free," Caper said to me. "Because I think you really want to stay. Especially now that you know you have to." He was very casual, but very definite.

"But why do we have to?" I asked, half knowing the answer, but wanting someone to say it.

"So you won't give us away," Caper said.

Yes, that was the danger, of course. But now at last, my two-sided mind was completely made up. Much as I liked Ariel, I had no intention of staying. I would go along with Caper now, so I would not be held prisoner. Only if I were free, did Waver and Bisty have a chance of being set free. And they would be, if I could possibly manage it. The three of us would take the ship home. If we really wanted to, we could do it.

We were led off into the forest at once. The three men were joined by a group of others, and Waver and Bisty were all but thrown into a cart with some of the animals we had killed. I did not look back as we started off. There was no point in reminding anyone that the ship was still there. And that one of us had the key— me! My mind began to work frantically. If we should be searched and the key was taken from me, our chances of leaving this place would be far smaller. I had to get rid of the key.

Running up to Caper, I pointed at the bushes. He understood what I meant, and so did the others. I ran back to a place near the path, and squatted down out of sight. There wasn't much time. But surely I could hide the key and mark the place somehow. I was behind a clump of bushes with a small tree growing out of the center. I dug a hole at the base of the tree and planted the key. Then I tore a piece from my underpants and tied it to the base of the bush, trying at the same time to memorize the location. We were not too far from the edge of the forest, and on what seemed to be a path. If I could find the path again, I should be able to find the key.

"Sorry," I muttered, dashing up to join the others. Actually, only Caper and Gloust had made any pretense of waiting; the men, with their carts, were moving slowly ahead in the distance.

"Where are we going?" I asked brightly.

"The others have a village in the forest," Gloust said companionably. "Caper and I haven't seen it. It's a couple of days away on foot. They saw us come down in the ship, and when they came for the animal run, they looked for us, too. Caper talked to them and said he wanted to stay and he thought we could be persuaded to stay, too."

"It's a great place," I said. "So beautiful. Are there a lot of people?"

"Quite a few," Gloust said. "They farm and have log houses. Been here ten, fifteen years. They all knew each other before, but I don't know if they all came together."

"The animals," I said. "Did you know?"

"Caper knew," Gloust explained. "But he didn't tell me. They come every year. Generally they're day animals, but when they go to the south like this, they move night and day. The men come to shoot them and dry the meat for food. It lasts them all year. At first they weren't too happy about us. But now that we're going to stay, it's all right. They don't have many children, and Caper told them they need us if the next generation is going to survive."

I couldn't believe that Gloust could actually accept all that. Yet, I decided, he really might like to be one of twenty, or thirty at most, who would one day inherit a planet. He liked exploring the wild. It had always been what he wanted. Still, even for him, I would think it would be a bit lonely—cut off from good things as well as bad. A backwash that time and civilization would ignore.

"I think all of you will like it, once you get used to the idea," Caper said. "After all, we are Earth people, and Earth's heritage is freedom and isolation, keeping the beauty of the world around you."

I knew I should agree. "Yes, that's true," I said mechanically. But was it? Was Earth our only heritage? Hadn't our parents, or grandparents, left Earth to build

140

another heritage—a heritage of travel to far places and an acquiring of knowledge that Earth valued but did not want as a part of its immediate way of life?

And Earth was not backward. For all its deliberate isolation, it made a contribution to the galactic union. People did come and go. There were retreats and convocations and peace meetings on Earth all the time. Earth served a purpose. But did this planet? We would be living our lives alone, cut off from everyone, getting nothing, giving nothing. If it were necessary, that would be one thing. But when it wasn't, it seemed a bleak and lonely future.

"Ariel is a lovely place," I said again, to cover my turmoil. "By the way, what do these people call it?"

"Oh, they've never given it a name that I know of," Caper said vaguely. "Maybe they'll like Ariel. They're too busy for things like names, I guess. You'll see why when you get to the village. I know it will be a place you'll like." He patted me on the shoulder and walked forward to talk to one of the men pulling the cart that held Waver and Bisty.

My mind was in a panic. This was mad! Mad! We were too young to be so isolated. Why hadn't I seen that before! And we all had a right to make choices about our lives. The people who lived here had come because they wanted to. And they had come after they had learned and lived and seen the galaxy. We had had no such opportunities, and we were being given no choice in the matter of staying. It was not fair.

I suddenly thought again about my parents. It seemed probable now that they had gone to some place like this, in a time when self-space-placement had been freer. But they had not taken me. Why? So that I could make choices! It was perfectly obvious. They had loved me and had cared enough to see that my future would not be limited by what they had decided was best for them. A great feeling of love and determination spread over me. If they had cared that much, then I had to do whatever I could to keep faith with their hopes for me.

But how to get away? Bisty and Waver, at least, would be carefully watched. And I was sure the men would also keep an eye on me, and perhaps even Gloust, no matter how eager he was to be a part of the group. I walked on, keeping an eye on everything, ready to take whatever chance turned up. And trying to anticipate what that chance might be.

13

It was midday when we were taken off into the forest. And we did not stop walking until the day was nearly over. The pace was slow, but it was continuous. The path we took was long, and as straight as the forest would allow. There were few branch paths, and all seemed to lead to a stream or sometimes to what appeared to be caves in a line of low hills to the left, beyond a narrow river.

I kept my eyes open, alert to changes in the path, to any side paths that might prove troublesome if one wanted to go back the same way.

The end of the day's journey finally came when we reached a steam that seemed to feed into the river at the left. It was not a large stream, but I could see that it would be difficult to pull the wagons across because it was muddy and full of weeds at the bottom.

"Better stop here," one of the men said. It was almost

143

the first time I had heard one of them talk. His speech sounded like ours, but there was an accent, a slurring of the words, that made the overall rhythm different. It stood to reason that over a period of years there would be changes, but it made me wonder what other changes had taken place.

The man began to make a fire and took bags of meat from one of the carts to cook. Waver and Bisty were left in their cart. I hated to think of how they must feel. I wondered if I could have stood being bumped along that rocky path, bundled up in a heavy bag.

"What about *them*?" one of the men asked finally, a certain contempt in his voice.

From what Gloust had said, I had thought we might be welcomed to the enclave; but the man's voice made me doubt it.

"Better take them out and let them lie flat on the ground," Caper said. "We'll feed them and give them something to drink later."

Neither Bisty nor Waver moved as the men lifted them and dumped them on the ground. They had been more careful with the bags of meat.

Gloust, when I gave him a quick glance, was looking troubled. Obviously things were not going as he had thought they would.

Several men had been holding pieces of meat on sticks near the fire to cook. It smelled good, but I was not sure I wanted any. And it was a good thing I felt that way because I was given only a small piece. I picked some plants nearby that I knew were edible and made most of my meal on them. Caper paid little attention to me, but Gloust, whose piece of meat was only a little larger than mine, gave me an unhappy look.

It was then that I first began to have a real hope that we would be four going home, not three. Though I didn't dare to count on Gloust yet.

Just before we all lay down for the night, Caper and another man opened the bags and gave Waver and Bisty some water. The two said nothing, but they did swallow the water. So they were conscious. That would help if the chance came to get away. And to my relief, they were not put back in the bags, though they were tied hand and foot.

What did I have that was sharp? Nothing. No! I had the small knife I had used that morning when Bisty and I had gathered food. It was still buttoned in my pocket, I thought. Yes. Small. Not very sharp. But better than nothing.

As I looked around for a place to spend the night, a place where I would not be seen if I got up—or at least not heard, because I would be seen if someone woke up—I saw Gloust come near. Was he going to insist on sleeping close by? I pretended to be glad to see him, but I didn't know if I was or not. There was still no way to be sure which side he was on.

"I'm really tired," I said. "I hope we get there tomorrow, or that we take more rests. I'm not used to this, even after all the walking we've done."

He gave me a bleak smile. "It's that soft living," he said. "But you'll get over it. This is a healthy life, out in the open."

Caper had obviously overheard. He looked at us now and grinned. "A week or two of the good life, and you'll be ready for anything."

I smiled back. "I hope so. I wouldn't want to miss out, just because I'm not ready." I meant that in more ways than I hoped he understood.

One other man glanced over casually, but didn't seem interested in us. The rest ignored us completely. None of them seemed to be the sort of men who would have driven spaceships. But then, of course, they had been on Ariel a long time. They had become adjusted to the kind of life they had to live here—primitive. And we would adjust, too. But right then I didn't want, or intend, to.

I stretched out on a soft place on the ground with a bed of leaves, as many as I could pull together easily, beneath me. It was not comfortable. So I wouldn't have to worry about going to sleep.

If I hadn't been alert, every nerve awake, I would never have noticed Gloust moving closer. As it was, I held myself still and waited to see what he would do.

"Don't move," came his soft whisper. "Don't turn." It was so low a voice I was sure no one else had heard. We were a good dozen meters from the group around the fire. Obviously we were trusted. Or they had such contempt for our physical condition they didn't think we would try to get away.

"I got you into this, or at least I helped, and I'm going to get you out."

I wanted to trust him, but I didn't know if I dared.

"Listen, I don't believe for a minute that you want to stay here. You were just being smart. Smarter than Caper thought you would be. There was a bag for you, too, you know. He believes you want to stay because he can't accept anyone's wanting to leave."

146

"Don't you want to stay?"

"I did. But that was before I saw how it would be. Those guys, they aren't human anymore. I walked beside some this afternoon. They don't talk; they don't even seem able to think. I don't want that to happen to me. I like this place, but not that much. Besides, I don't like the way they treated Bisty."

He had seen the men just as I had seen them, then. Maybe you couldn't cut yourself off this way and stay human, or at least stay very intelligent.

"Listen," Gloust whispered again, "you've got to believe me. When I say go, you go. It will mean all the others are asleep. Follow the path. Get the ship ready. I'll bring the others. The men won't suspect me if they see me up, the way they might suspect you."

What he said was true. And I knew suddenly that I could trust him. He was, after all, one of The Terrible Four. We had been together since we were little more than babies. What had happened to Waver and Bisty had to have bothered him in a way that even Caper would not understand. And adding to that, there was the absence of dessert energy-bars! I almost laughed. Yes, I could trust Gloust.

I murmured a soft yes, then pretended to be almost asleep as he rolled a little ways away. A few minutes later, Caper came over to see us again. As far as he was concerned, we were both asleep. He moved back to the fire and the other men.

"Those two all right?" I heard a man ask.

"Sound asleep," Caper said. "These kids are soft. But they'll toughen up."

"Have to," said the man. "What about the ship?"

147

"Leave it for now," Caper said. "One of the kids must have the key if it's locked. But they can't go anywhere. I tinkered with the guidance system, broke a couple of parts. So even if they should get back there, which they won't, they can't take it out. If we want to move the ship to a more protected place, I can always fix it."

That was Caper, our Caper. Why did he want this life so much? But then why did any Discoverers want it? Did something inside all of us cry out for a place of beauty, a chance to be out of doors, a sense of freedom? Did we all need wind and grass and sun and rain? Maybe. And in the present setup, for Discoverers, this was the only way to get it.

I shoved a stone under my hip, to make sure I wouldn't go to sleep; but even so, I almost did. The fire had died down completely, and I could hear some fierce snoring from around its embers when Gloust's soft but piercing whisper brought me suddenly wide awake.

"Now!" he said. "Quiet."

I did not move at once. But when no one else stirred, I gradually slid along the ground as if I were moving in my sleep. I pushed a little way, then rolled a little, then stopped to listen. There was no sound but the snoring. So I moved a little more. And then a little more. Finally I pulled myself to my hands and knees, crawled to the shelter of a large tree and looked back. Gloust was watching me, but everyone else was asleep.

Could he rescue the others? I hoped so. I had to count on it. I drew myself slowly to my feet, peered again at the sleeping men, then set off down the dark path. It would not be easy to find my way in the night. I had no light. And suddenly I remembered that I had hidden the key. I would have to find it again before any of us could get into the ship. And the hiding had all been for nothing. They hadn't searched any of us. I was amused that Caper had never discovered that I had fixed the guidance system. Actually he didn't realize that I was capable of it or had the necessary tools. He had underestimated us all the way. And he had known us so well! But then we had thought we knew him, too.

The path proved easier to follow then I had thought it would be, simply because the forest was so dense on either side. You couldn't leave the path without knowing it. Eventually, although I was tired, I began to run. There was a long way to go, and there was always the chance that someone would discover I had escaped. In any case, we only had until morning before the men would be out looking for us. And they would know that none of us could find our way back except by the path. The thought gave my feet rockets. I all but flew, ignoring the roughness of the ground, the occasional stones, and the fact that I was dead tired and scared. Scared both of what lay behind and what might be around and ahead of me in the forest.

I don't know how long I ran. Eventually I wasn't even conscious of moving. I just went: sometimes bumping into a tree, sometimes stumbling and almost falling, but always going on, hands in front, arms waving ahead to find the path, to find the curves when they came. There were narrow branch paths now and then, but these I knew I could ignore. I had to keep to the main route.

At last the thick forest eased a little, and the light of the moon broke through. I slowed a bit then. But did not stop. To stop would be to give up. I had the feeling that only if I kept moving could I continue to go on.

Then finally I glanced up and thought I saw the end

of the forest in the far distance. It seemed impossible that I had already come so far, though we had walked at a slow pace in the afternoon. If anyone had told me then that I could run all the way back, I would have laughed. You can do what you have to do, they had always told us at the School/Home. And now I believed it.

The key, I remembered then! I must be near the place I had put it. But darkness hid the configurations of bushes and trees, and certainly would hide a small piece of cloth tied to a branch. Yet I had to find that key. Just how far had I been from the edge of the forest? How had it all appeared? I really slowed then, wanting to remember. I had imprinted the location on my mind, but things looked so different at night. I grew nervous. Surely someone was following me—would catch up with me now and find me. I made myself stop. There was no sound behind me, no walking or running. Only the mysterious sounds of the forest, which I preferred not to hear.

Calm down, I said, almost aloud. Talking to myself! I almost laughed aloud. I could just hear Waver commenting on my mental state. And that made me sad. He thought I had betrayed him. And in some ways I had. Yet it was my indecision then that was making escape possible for all of us now.

What was happening with the others? There was no time to wonder. I quieted, then concentrated on what I had done earlier. I made the landmarks I had set in my mind reappear. Then I tried to imagine them in the near dark. We had been trained to do that. I hadn't been much good at it, not the way Waver was; but now when I needed it, some of it came back to me.

Not quite there yet, I thought. I moved ahead slowly. No, not quite yet. But near. Another few steps. There, that seemed right. It would be to the left side now. I moved off the path, looking for bushes, a small tree in the middle.

Nothing looked right. I made myself quiet again, looked at the path, at the end of the path where it merged into the moonlit plain. Yes, this had to be about right.

I let my eyes accustom themselves to the dark of the forest again. Then I tried to pick out configurations of growth. There—was that it? No, not quite right. I moved to the side of the path. How far into the forest had I gone? I stood and glanced around. Was that it? Maybe! No, not there. But over there?

I moved toward a clump of bushes with a small tree in the center. Forced my way into the branches, not caring how scratched I became. Was there a piece of cloth? Yes! This was the place! I could hardly believe it. Feverishly I dug into the ground. Here? No, a way over. Yes, the ground felt soft, different. And there at last was the key. I had found it. Against all reason, I had found it.

I stood up once again. Listened. No sounds of pursuit. So near now. I had to make it.

Back on the path. Running again. It didn't matter how tired I was, I had to do it. Not only for me, for the others. I had to have the ship open and ready to go when they came. If there was no one after me, there might well be someone after them.

The edge of the forest at last, the hill beyond, the shelter which only last night—could it be only last night?—had been knocked from its base by that vast herd of animals. Around the hill, and then, the ship. It was still there! Dark and quiet. Seeing it was an enormous relief, though I knew no one could have taken it away.

I moved quietly and carefully now. It was an open plain, with no vegetation left. No place to hide. I bent close to the ground and moved in what I hoped were deceptive patterns. Just in case. I didn't want to be seen from either the forest or the ship. At the same time, I used a stick I had picked up at the edge of the forest to knock away my footprints. Just a precaution. It took longer that way, but it seemed safer.

I was afraid to approach the door of the ship when I drew near. What if someone was there? What if someone was hiding in the shadows, just waiting for me to come and let him in?

But there was no one outside. I quickly opened the door, stepped in, closed the door, and locked it behind me. I had done it!

I sank to the floor at the foot of the short flight of steps up to the second air lock, wondering if I would ever get up again. I wanted to go to bed, but I knew I could not. There was too much to be done. I had to get the ship ready for takeoff. We would be four under the helmets—four very tired persons. Sitting, I let my mind move ahead. Close all the ports. Secure all the protective gear except at the door and one or two viewports, so I could open them when I needed to see out. Get the helmets ready. And—yes, most important—find the nearest junction point with secure slips, regardless of whether it was on the way home or not. When we left, we would not go to a planet. I had had enough of planets. But we would have to go someplace where we could all rest.

Wearily I rose from the floor and pulled myself up into the cabin. I closed the ports and then turned on the lights, secured the outside with the protective devices, but left the door and a port on either side clear. Made the helmets ready. Then to the charts. There was a junction point about three-quarters of an hour away in Sector 23. The wrong direction, but the closest place. I put the chart and all the factors in front of the helmets, so we would have them to follow and could get where we were going no matter how tired we were. And then there was nothing to do but wait.

Again, I was afraid to sleep. Once asleep, I might not awaken to let the others in when they came. And the whole advantage of my being there would be lost.

I don't really believe in taking drugs, though everyone does it. I hate how they make me feel. But I knew I couldn't avoid them this time. I went to our medical supplies and took a pill that I hoped would keep me wide awake for as long as necessary. Then I turned out the lights in the command room, opened the port that faced the forest, and began to watch for my friends, all three of them.

14

In spite of the pill, I must have slept, because I found myself curled up on the floor by the port with the light pouring in. Did it never rain on this planet? It must, with everything so green, but when? It was ironic to wonder about such a thing when my friends were in danger, when I might have put us all in further danger by falling asleep. But my mind didn't want to touch that. It was easier to think of sun and rain.

I pulled myself up to the port, stiff and sleepy. It must have been the light that awakened me, because when I opened the port to the east, the sun was still low in the sky. I couldn't have slept long. Scanning near the barren ground and the edge of the forest to the west, I saw no sign of life. Could the three be down at the door where I couldn't see them?

I crept through the upper air lock, down the stairs,

and knocked softly at the inside of the door to see if I would get a response. There was no answer. But where were they? What condition were Waver and Bisty in? Was it possible they were so exhausted they couldn't walk? And they had had nothing to eat, only something to drink, I remembered. What had happened when Gloust freed them?

Was it possible that they had all been caught again? I knew it was, much as I hated to admit it. And I couldn't begin to think about what I should do if they didn't come.

I decided to look over the food supply and get the food and oxygen ready for a quick trip. All sorts of ideas whirled in my mind as I worked methodically to complete the job of getting ready for takeoff. Since I had done the essentials the night before, these basically housekeeping chores didn't take much thought.

When everything I could think of to do was done, I ate some of our stored food and moved to the charts. I didn't have as much knowledge of the area as Waver or Gloust, but I thought maybe I could find some nearby planet that I could reach by self-space-placement. What I hoped for was a sparsely settled planet that wouldn't have too many screens. Occupied by a space-roving people perhaps. Even to such a place a trip would be dangerous, because I didn't have the right kind of suit. Yet if I could find such a planet not too far away, I knew I would have to try to reach it if the others didn't come.

While I worked, part of my mind listened for a shout or even a gentle tap from the outside. And every few minutes I went to look. No one came. I would wait

155

through the day and the night, I decided. Then I'd make a decision about what to do. My search of the charts had produced nothing. Deep down I knew that it was either escape for the four of us by ship or face a lifetime on Ariel. But I wasn't ready to acknowledge that yet.

Late in the morning I slept again for a little while. And then sometime in the afternoon, on one of my visits to the viewport looking toward the west, I saw movement at the edge of the trees. I stood motionless before the port, waiting and hoping.

At first I thought I had been mistaken in thinking someone was there. A breeze in the low branches, perhaps. But then I saw a figure, one and then two. Were there three? I ran for the binoculars and trained them toward the forest. There were only two; no, there were three; no, four. And they were not the ones I had hoped for. It was Caper and three of the men. Without thinking, I pushed the button that closed the shield over the door. Then I cursed myself. Now they would know that someone was in the ship. Though they didn't have binoculars. Maybe they wouldn't have seen the small movement. There seemed to be no response. Yet the very fact that the shield was closed would indicate that someone had to be there. I opened it a crack again—a very small crack, as if we had just slipped out at the last.

The men did not seem to notice. They stood looking at the ship, but they were not excited, not as excited as they would be if they had proof that we were there. Then it occurred to me that the ship might not be here at all if the four of us had arrived together. And they might not know that I had escaped ahead. So if they were there looking, waiting, the others had gotten away and had not been caught. It was a trap!

Now I was really upset. The men had probably had some sleep. But Waver and Bisty and Gloust would have had none. They would be no match for the men, especially if the trap came as a surprise. But there was no way I could warn them, not without giving away my own position. And my presence in the ship was obviously an advantage if speed in getting in was necessary.

I went back to my charts, still looking halfheartedly for ways home for one. But what was happening on Ariel was of much more concern to me.

On another of my frequent visits to the port, I saw that the men were moving. At first I couldn't tell if they were coming to the ship or not, but then I knew that they were. What was bringing them here? The ship's shield could be locked in any position, but I had not locked it in case the others should come and I might want to open it a little more. I glanced hastily around to make sure the three were nowhere near, then locked the shield with its small opening and made sure the door behind was also locked.

The men moved slowly, talking and gesturing as they came. They didn't seem to have any purpose in their movements, so I decided they were just coming to check out the ship. I crept down near the locked door and, because the shield outside was open a little, I could hear them.

"Locked, of course," Caper said. "It's natural."

"Can break in sometime if we need to," one man said.

"But I suppose we'll get the key when we take them again."

"You're sure you don't know where they are, that you're not a part of some plan," another said to Caper.

"I told you," he answered, "I was sure of those two, especially the boy. I thought he camped over by the girl to make sure she didn't do anything. He was ready, I tell you."

"Can't be too sure," said one. "Can't be sure of you, maybe. A plot. Have to be careful. Too good a place to lose. Free and empty."

"Listen." Caper sounded desperate. "I've wanted this for years. And the trip with these kids seemed a perfect chance. I landed here once, with a five party; made them take off almost right away because I had a sense that someone was here. I knew, of course, what was happening everywhere, and I wanted it, too. Never reported anything about this planet. The other four forgot we'd even been here. Told 'em it was a poison planet. And they believed me."

"Hope we can believe you," said another voice. "Know how 'tis though. But why not come alone? Why bring the kids?"

"You've been away too long," Caper said. "You can't do that anymore. Too many screens to use self-space-placement. And the trips I go on are never in small ships. Too many people to do anything off the schedule. The kids were the only way. And I didn't dare plan too much, tell them too much, for fear I was wrong—that there was no one here. I had to be careful. I had to leave myself room to go back in case I didn't find you. After all, four kids and a man couldn't survive alone, even in a place like this. Yet it ought to have worked. It will still work. . . ." He drifted off, as if suddenly he wasn't quite sure. The others were quiet, and I didn't know what they felt.

I didn't know what I felt. So Caper had planned this. From how far back, I wondered. Was the whole idea of these trips his? Or had he simply used them? And how much of our troubles had he created? Certainly the details of this survival trip were his. And he was perfectly willing to sacrifice us to his desire to stay here. He had said a couple of days ago that selfishness was not the greatest sin in the galaxy, and obviously he believed it. Had all his kindness to us over the past couple of years been only to gain his own ends? That didn't seem likely, but I couldn't be sure.

I wanted to cry, but I didn't dare. The men were still outside.

"Nothing here," one of them said finally.

"I didn't think there would be," Caper said. "They couldn't have been gone long when we woke up. And none of them was in any state to travel far."

Obviously Caper didn't know what you could do when you had to. I grinned to myself. Maybe he didn't know a lot of things.

"Too hot here," another man said. "And they'll see us if they come. Better to hide in the forest."

I was glad to see them go, but knew that the danger was greater for Gloust and the others with the men in the forest. I hoped they would be careful. But of course they would be. We might not know all of the dangers that lay in those trees, but we knew how to deal with dangers we understood. Gloust had been with Caper.

159

He would know what to expect. And Waver was always good at planning. They would come, all three of them. And we would survive. More than that, we would get away.

15

The day was gone, and the night had come. But not total darkness. The moon that had helped me the night before had not yet risen, but two small moons we had not seen before—maybe because we had slept while they were up—were showing themselves over the horizon. They threw odd patterns of light over the plain. A few clouds had begun to gather in the sky, and their shadows, long in the low moonlight, made a network of light and dark that delighted me.

The four men were still in their place on the western side of the plain. I could see them now and then with my binoculars. They had made a small fire to cook by and evidently were enjoying a late dinner. I supposed they would sleep, but that someone would be left on watch. Night would be the best time for the others to come, though, and I had to be ready. I took another wake-up pill, hoping it would do more for me than the first one. Actually, I had had a number of short naps during the day, and I didn't feel too tired. Maybe because I was so tense. If the others didn't come tonight, I would have some difficult decisions to make.

Three of the men did go to sleep after they ate, and a fourth stood watch. He walked up and down, probably to stay awake, and kept his eyes on the edge of the forest.

The two small moons were high in the sky, and the moon of the night before was just rising when I went to look out the port to the east, as I had several times before. It was a relief to look at a landscape where there were no men searching for us. The forest there seemed a long way away, beyond the plain and the area of shrubby growth. Yet actually it probably wasn't more than two kilometers. We had walked it a number of times. Even carried water from there. But we had not explored it as completely as we had the western woods.

As I examined the area with my binoculars, wondering what those trees hid, I thought I saw movement among the bushes. I trained the glasses on the spot. Was someone there? More men? The shifting patterns of clouds and tree shadows made the area difficult to see. Any movement might be wind among the bushes.

Yet I began to believe I saw three figures!

But why from the east? How did they get there?

When I thought it over, it made sense. The west was being watched. Gloust, at least, would expect that. The forest on the west connected to the forest on the north, where the animals had come from. And that forest led to the one on the east. It was a long way around, but a safer approach.

162

It was a perfect night for crossing the plain unseen, I realized. For the first time since we had come, there were clouds and cloud shadows. Maybe it was the end of a dry season and the beginning of a rainy one. Which must be why the animals had appeared! They must arrive at this time every year, eating the ripe fruit and tall grass along the way, and going to the south, to the plains there, or perhaps beyond, when bad weather approached.

I kept myself busy thinking and not looking, not wanting to trust my eyes too much. I could be wrong. And to be too sure and then be mistaken would be shattering. Yet when I looked again, I was certain I saw them. They were keeping low. Moving in uneven patterns, staying within the cloud shadows. Slipping on, then resting, or hiding more likely, stretching out flat on the denuded ground.

Very cautiously I opened the shield a little more. Not enough that even a watcher in the daytime would notice. And I unlocked the door so that it could be opened quickly. They were halfway across the plain. It would become more dangerous as they drew nearer. They were separated now. Coming slowly on. Still keeping to cloud patches, moving as the shadows moved.

Then at last they were at the rear of the ship. One of them knocked very lightly, and I knocked back. Then nothing.

What were they waiting for? I looked at the larger moon, just above the trees to the east. They must want its shadow to protect them at the door. But they couldn't wait too long or the small moons would light the door. They were just about overhead.

I moved down the steps, ready to open the door at the first sound. And just as I got there, it came. A very gentle knock. "Gloust," I murmured.

"Waver," came the reply.

I slipped the door open a crack, and he slid in, took my hand and squeezed it hard, but said nothing. He was followed at slight intervals by Gloust and Bisty. Before any of us even said hello, I locked the door, then ran up the steps and completely closed the shield.

Actually we didn't say anything for a long few minutes. We just sat in the dark delighting in each other's presence.

Then finally Waver said, "Whew, were we glad to hear that knock on the other side. We were afraid you hadn't made it. And we knew you had the key. Good work, old girl. Couldn't have done better myself."

It felt good to laugh. "But how did you get over to the east?" I asked at last. "How did you find your way? That was a long way to go. And you must have been exhausted."

"Elementary. Tonight, when we could see the sky, we used those constellations we made up to guide us. And all day we simply hid in one of those caves. Gloust, as you will remember, had once before proposed them as a place of residence. And he was quite right. Though not really comfortable enough for long-term living, they were better than carts."

"Oh, that's enough, Waver," Gloust said. "Don't rub it in. I was a fool, and I admitted it. And it was a good idea to rest and get some sleep."

"Gloust, you are an absolute hero," Bisty said. "You and Rom. We could never have done it without you. And Waver knows it's true."

164

"Yes, but what I don't understand is how Rom knew what was about to happen so she didn't get bagged up the way we did."

"I'll tell you about that someday," I said. "Right now, we've got to get out of here."

We closed the ports. I showed them the plans I had made, and they agreed that we should go to the junction in 23. None of us was ready for a long jump. And everyone wanted a good stable place to rest and plan, something that wasn't a planet.

"Let's go!" Waver said, as soon as they'd all looked at the charts and had a little to eat.

We turned out the lights, opened the ports, and slipped in under the helmets by moonlight. It took us longer than usual to fasten each other in, because we hadn't done it in a while and because we were excited and tired. But once we were in, the old accord was there. I could feel the concord of our minds meshing with the guidance system, and our lift was very smooth. My only regret was that I couldn't watch Caper and his friends as the ship disappeared before them.

The flight took a little longer than it should have. And we had a little trouble docking, a maneuver that had never bothered us before. But we got in, took off our helmets, shook hands all around and disappeared to our bunks. My last thought was that Waver had been right: None of us had realized before this trip how much of Discovery was just sleeping.

16

We arrived home at the very time we were expected. Which amazed all four of us. We had long since stopped thinking about our instructions. From the junction point in 23, we had plotted a leisurely course of short hops from one junction point to another, so that we never had to hold the ship ourselves. This took us out of our way, but we felt it was worth it. We rationed our food and water, and it lasted long enough. But we had decided that if we ran out, we would simply get some provisions at a junction point. We would have to bill it to the school, but we didn't care. We had had enough of survival on our own.

A small crowd came to the dock at the School/Home as soon as people realized we were there. Obviously they had been waiting for us. Maybe they had been looking for us since the day we left. I'm sure most of the teachers, at least, had felt we were unprepared.

The only reason why they hadn't worried about us was that Caper was with us. That's what the Head said, when he shook hands all around. And only then did he notice that Caper wasn't there.

Before we did anything else, we asked for a private talk with him, and told him our whole story. To sum up, he was impressed by what we had done. After all, we had not only fulfilled all the rules that the committee had set, we had fulfilled Caper's secret rules as well. And no one could fault us for undertaking such a hazardous trip. Everyone at the School/Home had trusted Caper, too.

After we had unpacked and settled into our old pod, there were long discussions with faculty groups. No one blamed us for anything that had happened. And best of all, the future began to look better than we could have hoped. We had been promised "advanced studies" if we succeeded. And obviously we had. Once we had believed those advanced studies would simply give us a further chance to lose ourselves in space. But instead we found that we were actually going to be able to plan our studies and move in whatever directions we chose.

No more Keery Soter. No more dull routine courses just because they were required. Waver could swallow Earth's whole past at once if he could manage it, even if no one could predict what he would do with it. Bisty could try out all kinds of ideas for new life-support systems. Gloust could have his fill of advanced space exploration techniques, along with a chance to work out ideas on controlled colony planting—even if Earth didn't plant colonies. I could study ship design and repair on whatever kinds of ships I chose. But that didn't really satisfy me. I had become more like Waver, and the idea of doing the same thing all the time filled me with dread.

It was the log that provided at least a part of the answer to what else I could do. I had kept everything up-to-date, and at the Head's request, after we had talked with him, made a copy of it and wrote a summary report.

"You should learn to be a recorder," the Head said, when he looked over what I had done. "You're obviously good with machines, and you should have more training in that. But your ability with records is special. We need reports like this because they can help others see and feel what an experience is like, not just encounter dull statistics. In fact, your log is just what I needed right now."

What he meant was that he had some ideas he wanted to present to the All-Earth Council. Earth had, of course, been notified of what had happened to us and what we had found on Ariel. No one had been sent there. There seemed to be no point in doing so. Those people, even Caper, were doing what they wanted to do, and they were not hurting anyone. Best to let them stay where they were. But also, best not to let good people slip away like that if it could be prevented. The galaxy needed their talents.

The Council met right here on Meniscus F so we could attend and tell our story in person. Out of it came the decision that some colonizing will be done by Earth. A few good planets will be absorbed into the Earth system, as a refuge for those who have left Earth or—like us—share an Earth heritage though they have never been to Earth. These planets will be as wild and free as possible. Yet they will welcome anyone who wants to come, and will allow those who do come to develop and use themselves and their skills to the fullest. Anyone in Discovery or at any Earth base for any reason will be allowed to go—for a brief time or for a lifetime. And Earth people can go, too, if they want.

It's an exciting prospect, and it opens the door for Waver and his assorted knowledge, for Gloust and his colonizing plans, and for anyone else who may not fit the usual Discovery pattern. I may want such a life myself.

In the meantime, we Discoverers extraordinary are content at the School/Home—almost. We are once again The Terrible Four. And, as always, we work hard to keep things moving. Yet there are still problems. We don't meet much opposition anymore. Sometimes it seems we can do no wrong, no matter how outrageous we become. It spoils all the fun of being outrageous. But more than that, three octaves and two pauses without dessert-energy bars created a physical situation that cannot be completely reversed. We are no longer a part of the middle group. Nor are we ready in other ways for the older group. In other words, we have become more isolated than ever before.

Our common room, for we still share a pod, remains a gathering place—but more for those of any age who yearn for the new than for our old age-mates. We are the same, but not the same. We are glad for what we have had, yet sometimes we regret it. We have missed a part of our growing up and we know it—some years of indecision and special fun. Still, we know each other and, especially, ourselves far better than we might have, had we never moved out of the expected pattern.

We are a new breed, we sometimes tell ourselves, we

169

four: the vanguard of those with an Earth heritage who understand that they are not of Earth, not of one planetary heritage alone, but of the galaxy. The wonder of this is strong in us, and exciting. Yet the galaxy is a large place, and it can be a very empty place, a place for getting lost in. And I often wonder if it will ever hold another place for any of us that will be as full of delight as those first few days on Ariel. Because I am incurably hopeful, I believe it will. But that discovery may be a long way down a future that sometimes looks almost too big, even for fantastic adventurers like us.